MEET THE GIRL TALK CHARACTERS

Sabrina Wells is petite, with curly auburn hair, sparkling hazel eyes, and a bubbly personality. Sabrina loves magazines, shopping, sleepovers, and most of all, she loves talking to her best friends.

Katie Campbell is a straight-A student and super athlete. With her blond hair, blue eyes, and matching clothes, she's everyone's idea of Little Miss Perfect. But Katie has a few surprises for everyone, including herself!

Randy Zak has just moved to Acorn Falls from New York City, and is she ever cool! With her radical spiked haircut and her hip New York clothes, Randy teaches everyone just how much fun it is to be different.

Allison Cloud is a Native American Indian. Allison's supersmart and really beautiful. But she has one major problem: She's thirteen years old, five foot seven, and still growing!

SABRINA AND THE CALF-RAISING DISASTER

By L. E. Blair

GIRL TALK® series created by Western Publishing Company, Inc.

Western Publishing Company, Inc., Racine, Wisconsin 53404

Text by Susan Sloate

Chapter One

"That is the dumbest-looking donkey I've ever seen," said Randy Zak, pointing at a donkey poster tacked to the side of the barn. "Come on, Jason, it looks like somebody gave it a Mohawk haircut! You don't really expect me to pin a tail on that thing, do you?"

Jason McKee went closer to the barn to examine the poster. It was his barn and his poster — and his birthday party. That's why we were all standing in line with donkey tails in our hands, waiting to play pin the tail on the donkey.

It was actually a really cool party. Jason had invited a lot of great people, like my friends Katie Campbell, Allison Cloud, and Randy, plus my brother Sam and his friends Nick Robbins, Billy Dixon, and Arizonna Blake. There were also some annoying people there, like Stacy Hansen and her friends Laurel

1

Spencer, Eva Malone, and B. Z. Latimer, but in general it was a fun group. I'm Sabrina Wells, by the way, and we're all in the seventh grade at Bradley Junior High.

The other neat thing about the party was that it was taking place on Jason's family's farm. Jason lives on a farm right outside of Acorn Falls. He's the only kid I know at Bradley who has real farm chores to do before he comes to school in the morning.

Jason checked out the poster and turned around. "It's fine, Randy," he called. "Come on, don't chicken out on us."

"I am *not* chickening out!" Randy exclaimed.

"She's just afraid she won't do as well as I did," said my brother Sam, sounding smug. He looked at his own donkey tail, which he'd pinned at the side of the barn. It wasn't exactly on the donkey, but it wasn't *too* far off.

"Everybody knows boys have better natural balance and a better sense of direction than girls," Sam's friend Nick added. Nick's got blond hair and beautiful blue eyes. Usually I think he's really cute. Right now, though, I just thought he was acting dumb.

Randy stared at them for a minute, then

marched over and grabbed the blindfold from Jason. "Come on, you bingo heads. I'll show you who's better!"

I watched while Randy got blindfolded. Randy's from New York City and is cooler than anyone I know. It was weird watching her being spun around and pushed toward the donkey poster. Aside from having no idea where she was going, she looked really funny with a blindfold over her spiked black hair. She was wearing black Capri pants and a black turtleneck under a spangled black-and-purple sweatshirt.

Randy weaved around for a while, once almost bumping into a big oak tree right in the middle of the yard. Finally, though, she managed to get to something solid and stuck her donkey tail right in it.

"Hah!" she exclaimed, pulling off the blindfold. Then her big grin disappeared. She'd stuck her tail right into an unopened bag of potato chips on the picnic table! We all laughed out loud at that.

"Your turn, Sabs," Sam yelled as he grabbed me. "I'll bet you can't do any better. I'll bet you stick the tail right in the potato salad!"

Sometimes Sam can be so immature!

Jason tied the blindfold on me. "Hey," I complained, "you've got my hair in my eyes. I can't see!" My hair is auburn and curly and tends to get in the way.

"You're not supposed to see," Sam retorted. Somebody handed me a tail with a pin stuck in it, turned me around three times, and pushed me gently.

I couldn't see a thing and had no idea where the donkey poster was. I tried to keep going in a straight line, but I heard so much muffled giggling behind me, I was sure I had taken a wrong step somewhere.

I figured I must be getting close to the barn, and when I felt something solid in front of me, I stuck the tail right into it. Now the giggles got really loud. I pulled off the blindfold. I couldn't believe it! I'd stuck the tail right into a rug left drying on the clothesline!

I could see Allison and Katie laughing so hard, the tears were running down their faces. I couldn't help laughing, too. I had this sudden vision of the rug running around braying, with a paper tail on it. It really was funny.

"It's Katie's turn," Jason announced, head-

4

ing for Katie with the blindfold. Katie's long blond hair stayed neat, even when they tied the blindfold around it, and her jeans, white blouse, and mint-green sweater looked just as fresh as they had when she first walked into Jason's backyard.

I figured Katie would definitely hit the donkey. She's a terrific athlete. She's the only girl on the boys' hockey team at school and is even going to be the captain next year.

Katie weaved around just as much as Randy and I had. She finally pinned her tail just next to the big donkey poster. It was pretty close, a lot closer than Sam's, even. In fact, it was the best try yet.

It was Allison's turn next. She put her long, beautiful black hair behind her ears, and the boys reached up on tiptoes to tie on the blindfold. Allison was the tallest person at the party — she's already five foot seven!

The boys spun Allison around and set her off. I couldn't believe it! As soon as she got her balance, Allison made her way across the yard in a straight line and pinned her tail right on the donkey!

"Great job, Allison!" I yelled. "Nobody'll get

any closer than that!"

"That's what you think," Nick answered. At the beginning of the school year, I'd thought he liked me. Lately, though, he's been teasing me a lot. "Everybody knows boys are better at games than girls are!"

That infuriated me. "Prove it, Nick Robbins!" I challenged him. "I dare you!"

"Fine!" he yelled back. "Come on," he called to Jason. "Blindfold me!"

Jason put the blindfold on and spun Nick around a few times. Then Nick started walking with the donkey tail stuck way out in front of him. I could see exactly where he was headed, but I didn't say a word, and I did my best to smother the giggle rising in my throat.

"Ouch!" yelled Sam as Nick jabbed the donkey tail forward. "Cut it out! I'm no donkey!"

Everyone burst into roars of laughter as Nick pulled off his blindfold. He'd tried to pin his tail right on Sam, and Sam sure didn't appreciate it!

I could see Nick blushing. I felt a little sorry for him. It was true that he'd been out of line, but it wasn't nice to have everyone laughing at you. Maybe now he'd stop acting so puffed up and go back to being nice.

Just then Mrs. McKee called us all to come and get some food. She'd put out tons of wonderful goodies on a big picnic table, and we all took some to eat beneath the trees.

It was a terrific birthday lunch. There were fried chicken, potato salad, coleslaw, carrot and celery sticks, juices and sodas. And to top it all off, there was an amazing birthday cake. The cake had a farmyard scene on the top, with a stick figure that looked like Jason milking a cow. There were even a little barn and some other animals, too.

"Hey, Jason," Randy called as we all sat around stuffing our faces, "when can I see your horses? I hear you've got four."

"We do," Jason answered, licking his fingers. "I'll take you around afterward and show you. You can see the cows and calves, too, if you want."

"That sounds like fun," Allison said.

"Sure does," Katie agreed. "I'd like to come, too."

"Hey, Jason," said Billy, "are you entering Bradley's 4-H Fair?"

"Everybody's entering the fair," answered

Arizonna before Jason could say a word. "It's going to be one awesome day, dude."

"That's true," Stacy Hansen said quickly. "Of course, I already know who's going to win a blue ribbon."

My friends and I groaned silently. Stacy is the daughter of Mr. Hansen, Bradley's principal, and she thinks she's really cool. She's got long blond hair she's always tossing over her shoulder and really nice clothes. My friends and I call her Stacy the Great, and it's not meant as a compliment. For some reason the guys never seem to realize what a faker she is.

Jason nodded at Billy, who'd first asked the question. "I've got a calf I'm raising," he said proudly. "I think she'll do great."

That's one of the reasons I like Jason, even if he does hang around my brother Sam. He's really quiet most of the time, but he's nice, and he has a good sense of humor.

After lunch, Jason took most of the kids around the farm. It was really interesting to see all the machines and buildings. I never really knew before that farms had all those different things.

"And here are our horses," Jason said,

showing us into the stable. There were four beautiful animals, each in its own stall, with nameplates on the front.

Randy immediately went over to one of the horses and started petting him and talking to him. It was amazing. Randy is usually so tough and cool. But here she was, cooing to a horse, feeding him bits of carrots she had saved from lunch, even rubbing her spiked hair against his mane! Talk about a change!

Katie and Allison were getting into it, too. Katie was imitating Randy, petting the horse's mane. The horse seemed to like it. He made a funny sound in his throat and threw his head back. We all laughed.

Jason grinned as he watched them. Then he turned to me and asked, "Would you like to see my calf?"

"That sounds great," I said. I'd never seen a real calf up close.

We went outside to a small fenced-in pen. There were two black-and-white calves roaming around inside. Jason pointed to one. "That's him," he said proudly. "His name's Army."

"He's really pretty," I said. He was, too. He had big splotches of black and white all over his body.

Jason watched him proudly. "I've been working with him every day, teaching him to lead."

"What's that?" I asked.

"You have to teach the calf to walk around and stand and sit with a rope around its neck," Jason explained. "It's one of the competitions for calves at the fair."

I pointed to the other calf, the one he hadn't said anything about. "Who's that?" I asked.

Jason glanced over. "Oh" — he shrugged — "I'm not planning to enter her in the competition."

"Doesn't she even have a name?" I asked. I couldn't help thinking the poor little thing looked awfully cute. She gave me a kind of fast look out of her big brown eyes. Then she dipped her head down and looked at her hooves, like she was really shy. After a second she looked up again. I could swear she was actually winking at me!

She seemed to have a lot more personality than Jason's calf, even if she wasn't entered in the 4-H competition. "Doesn't she have a name?" I repeated.

Jason shook his head. "Why name a calf

you're not training?" he asked.

"That's terrible!" I said. "Everybody should have a name, at least. The poor thing looks so — so neglected!"

Jason burst out laughing. "Sabs, we feed her and take care of her just like all the other cows. She just isn't going to win any prizes, that's all."

"That's what you think!" I said hotly. "I'll bet this calf is just as smart as any calf you've got on this farm. I'll bet she could win all kinds of prizes if you'd just give her a chance!"

"Hear, hear!" cheered several voices behind me. Turning around, I saw Randy, Katie, and Allison. They'd come up behind us and were watching the little calf I'd found. Right behind them was Nick, who had this funny smile on his face.

"I'll bet Sabs could win a prize with that calf at the 4-H Fair," Randy said in a loud voice. She sounded so confident, I couldn't help feeling confident, too.

"Absolutely," Katie added. "She could train that calf to do anything."

Then Nick spoke up. "Oh, I don't know," he said. "The fair's only a few weeks away, and

Sabrina has no experience with farm animals. Besides, she'd have to come out here every day to feed it and train it."

I was furious! "I'll have you know, Nick Robbins," I said haughtily, "that just because I plan to be an actress doesn't mean I can't handle raising a calf. As a matter of fact, I might have to play a farm girl someday, so this would be a really good experience for me."

"No way," said Nick. "This isn't a movie, Sabs. This is a real animal."

Randy turned to Jason. "Well, Jason, what do you think?" she asked. "Could Sabs raise a calf by herself?"

"Sure she could," Jason answered. He didn't hesitate for a second. "In fact," he went on, "if she wants to try it, I'll ask my parents if she can raise this little calf and enter her in the 4-H Fair."

"Wow!" I shouted. "I'd love that! Thanks, Jason!"

I couldn't believe it! In one afternoon I'd gone from being Sabrina Wells, aspiring actress, to Sabrina Wells, farm girl and calf-raiser!

Chapter Two

The party ended in the late afternoon. Almost everyone had already gone home, but I wanted another look at my calf before I left. Jason had asked his parents if I could train her, and they said it would be fine. They'd keep her at the farm for me, but the calf's entire care, feeding, and training would be my responsibility from now on.

My friends and I went to see the calves. We hung over the pen. Already, my calf seemed to know me. "Don't worry about a thing," I reassured her, talking as softly as I could. "I'll be here every morning and after school to feed you. You won't miss a single meal."

Suddenly I heard a boy's voice behind me. "Well, that's a relief!" I looked up. It was Nick. I thought he'd left with the others. "I'd be afraid of starving to death if you were taking care of me," he said with a grin.

I couldn't believe him! "She won't have to worry about a thing," I said. "I'll do everything the way all the really scientific farmers do."

"How can you?" Nick asked. "You don't know what they do."

I hated to admit it, but he was right. It had just sort of slipped out.

Katie came to my rescue. "I'm sure that Sabrina can get some books at the library about scientific farming," she said.

"Yeah," said Randy, "not that she couldn't do it on her own, anyway."

"And I'm sure Jason would tell her if she was doing something really wrong," added Allison. "He wouldn't let her hurt her calf!"

My friends are the greatest! There was really nothing Nick could say now.

After we hung out with the calves for a little while, we all got ready to go home.

"Are you guys walking home?" Nick asked. He sounded a lot less confident now.

"No," I answered. "We rode our bikes."

"So did I. Let's all ride home together," Nick said.

Behind him I could see Katie and Randy whispering about something.

"Okay," I said. We said good-bye to Jason and got our bikes out of the driveway. As we started pedaling, I said out loud, "Now, the first thing is to get a really good name."

"For a calf?" Nick hooted. "Like what? Bessie?"

I read in *Young Chic*, my favorite magazine, that a person's name is really important in determining their personality. If a parent names a baby Sylvester or Murgatroyd, it can have a really damaging effect on the baby's life. Of course, that hadn't seemed to have hurt Sylvester Stallone any, but I didn't know any famous people named Murgatroyd. In fact, I didn't know anybody named Murgatroyd.

On the other hand, if a parent names a child David or Elizabeth, the child tends to be happier. Those are pretty common names, and it's easier to get along with people if you have a name that they already know.

I figured it was the same basic idea with a calf. I wanted to give my calf a really nice name, but it couldn't be something that would keep her from making friends with the other calves. On the other hand, I also wanted her to win the competition, so her name should show

how special and superior to the other calves she really was.

"Maybe . . . how about Florence?" I said. I hardly even realized I was talking out loud.

"Florence? For a calf?" Nick started to laugh so hard, I thought he was going to fall off his bike. As it was, it started wobbling around and everything. He grabbed the handlebars and slowed down so he could get control of it. "Florence Nightingale Calf!" he roared. "Perfect, Sabrina!"

I couldn't figure out why Nick made such a big deal of riding his bike home with us if all he wanted to do was insult me along the way. It wasn't such a silly idea to name a calf. I didn't feel like being laughed at anymore, so I didn't say anything else to him the entire way home.

That night I carefully set my alarm for five-thirty, because I had to get up, get dressed, and go to Jason's farm and do my chores before going to school. If I hurried, I would just have time to feed my calf and ride back in time for school at eight-thirty. My dad promised to drive me and my bike over in the morning, and Nick had said he'd come by and ride home with me in the evening. I guess he was trying to make up for hurting my feelings.

The next morning when the alarm rang, I couldn't move a muscle. Finally I thought about my poor calf going hungry and thirsty all day long while I was at school, and I jumped out of bed. I didn't think Jason would really let her starve, but I wanted him — and Nick — to know that I was responsible and mature.

It was just getting light when my dad dropped me off at the McKees'.

"Good morning," Jason said. "All set?" That's when I realized he did this every single day. No wonder he always seemed so energetic during first period. It had to feel like the middle of the day to him.

"All set," I answered, trying to sound more awake than I felt.

"Great," Jason told me. "Let's go feed the calves."

Jason led me into a big barn that had all kinds of lights and things rigged up inside. It looked really modern. "This is the dairy," Jason explained.

"You mean you actually milk these cows and get butter and stuff from them?" I asked. I always thought milk came out of cartons you bought in the supermarket.

Jason laughed. "Yep. This is where it comes from. We milk every day. Want to try it?"

"You mean I could milk a cow?" That was a pretty radical thought. I never got close to any animals at all, unless you wanted to count our dog, Cinnamon! But I was willing to take a shot. "Okay, sure," I said. "What do I do?"

Jason led me to a brown-and-white cow. She looked absolutely huge to me. "This is Alma," he explained. "She's one of our milk cows. She's really gentle. Come over here and sit down."

He showed me a small stool to sit on. Okay, I can handle this, I thought confidently. I'd seen those movies that had milkmaids leaning against cows and squirting milk into pails. I checked out the floor. Good, a tin pail. Okay. I pushed the pail under the cow.

"Great," Jason said, sounding surprised. "I thought you said you never milked a cow before."

"I haven't," I told him. "But this should be simple."

"Don't you want me to show you how?" Jason asked.

"Well, why don't you just tell me if I'm

doing something wrong," I said.

I sat down on the stool, leaning my head against the cow's side. She didn't moo or anything, so I guessed I was doing all right. I checked to be sure the pail was directly under her. It was. Then I reached for her udder.

I curled my fingers around her udder, but nothing seemed to happen. I was squeezing as hard as I could, but not a drop of milk was coming out.

"What is it?" I asked. "Maybe Alma doesn't have any milk today."

"You're not supposed to press on her like that," said Jason. "You look like you're trying to play the bagpipes or something. Here. Try it like this."

He leaned over and reached for what looked like little fingers sticking out of the udder. When he pulled on them and squeezed, milk squirted out.

That looked fairly simple. "Okay, I've got it now," I told Jason. He stepped away from Alma, and I started over, squeezing the milk into the pail.

Jason watched me for a few minutes. "That's really good," he told me finally.

"You've got the hang of it. Okay, then," he went on. "I want to start feeding the calves. So if you want to finish up here —"

I didn't want him to start feeding my calf, when I'd ridden all this way just to be with her. "No, it's okay," I said quickly, jumping to my feet.

Oh, no! I was in such a hurry to get up that I knocked over the stool, which banged against the tin pail. In a second the pail had tipped over, spilling out most of the milk I'd managed to squeeze into it!

"Oh, no. I'm sorry!" I cried.

Quick as lightning, Jason grabbed the pail and stood it up straight. There was still some milk in the bottom of the pail, but a lot was already gone. "No use crying over spilled milk," Jason said. "It's okay, Sabrina, really. Alma's not done milking, anyway. Come on, try it again."

Jason helped me clean up the milk that had spilled, and I milked Alma again. I had the whole procedure down this time, and we ended up with almost a whole bucketful. I felt pretty good about my new farm skills.

"Okay," Jason told me when I was finished.

"Now we can go feed the calves."

"That'll be great," I said happily. I couldn't wait to see my calf. I'd thought about her all night long. In fact, I'd even dreamed about her. It's a fact that you can make yourself dream about something if you think about it right before you go to sleep. In the middle of my dream, the best name had come to me. I knew right away that it was the perfect name for her.

Jason and I walked over to the pen where the two calves were already waiting for us. "Hi, Annabelle," I called to my calf.

"Annabelle?" Jason asked.

"Yep. That's her name," I told him. "Doesn't she look just like an Annabelle?"

Jason didn't answer that. He was busy hauling water to the long rectangular trough in the pen. "Fresh water, guys," he told them, dumping in the water. The calves came over right away and started lapping it up. "Come on, Sabrina," he told me. "We'll need grain. You can bring it in."

"Where is it?" I asked.

Jason nodded toward a little shed. "In there. Just scoop out a bucketful and bring it back."

I can do that, I told myself. "I'll be right

back, Annabelle," I told the calf. I didn't want her to think I was running out on her or anything. "Stay here. I'm getting you some great-tasting breakfast food."

I found a big empty bucket outside the shed and scooped up as much grain as I could. By the time I had the bucket full, I was almost staggering. I think the bucket weighed as much as I did! But I wanted Annabelle to be well fed. It wouldn't look good at the fair if I showed off a scrawny calf. So I hauled the bucket out to the pen.

Jason showed me the feed bin and helped me pour the grain into it. By this time my arms were aching. I hoped I'd develop some muscles before the fair. I had a feeling I was going to need them.

"What else do we do?" I asked when we had the water and grain set up.

Jason looked into another trough. "The calves need lots of hay," he explained. I checked the trough, too. There seemed to be plenty of hay in there already, but Jason lugged out an extra armful, just to be sure.

"Can I work with her while she's eating?" I asked him. I was really anxious to get started on my training program. After all, the fair was only a few weeks away, and I wanted to be ready.

"Why don't you just get used to each other for today?" Jason suggested. "She has to trust you before she'll work really well with you."

That was a good idea. Anyway, I wanted to try out a theory I had. I had an idea that you could raise a calf the same way some people raise plants. I've heard they actually name their plants and sing songs to them and talk to them. Nobody knows exactly why, but the plants grow really strong with that kind of treatment. I figured calves were like plants, except they had four legs and could walk around and moo. So I thought Annabelle and I would become a lot closer if I treated her like a plant.

"Hi, Annabelle," I cooed to her as she lapped up her breakfast. I saw Jason turn to me with a funny look on his face, but I didn't pay any attention. "Are you having a good breakfast? You've got some great grain and fresh hay to munch on. Does that taste good? I'll be coming out to feed you again after school."

Annabelle stopped munching for a minute and looked up at me. Of course, she didn't smile or anything, but I definitely had the feeling she knew what I meant. Anyway, she certainly looked interested.

I went a little closer to her and stuck my hand through the fence. "My name's Sabrina, but lots of people call me Sabs for short. I'm going to take care of you from now on. Okay?"

Annabelle looked at my hand and suddenly butted her head at my fingers. I was shocked. For a minute I thought she might even bite me. I quickly pulled my hand back.

"It's okay," Jason told me. "She's just getting to know you. Don't be afraid."

"Oh, I'm not afraid," I assured him. Actually, I was, a little, but I didn't think it would look very good if I admitted it. I was supposed to be turning Annabelle into a winner. I couldn't waste any time being scared of her.

To prove I wasn't afraid, I walked up to the pen again, holding my hand out a little nervously. Maybe it would be better if I soothed my calf by singing to her, I thought. Music relaxes a lot of people, so why shouldn't it work with animals?

I tried to think of something to sing. But I couldn't come up with a single song that seemed right. For some reason the only songs I could think of were the ones in the music videos Randy liked to watch, and I thought they'd scare Annabelle. That wasn't the idea at all.

While I stood there thinking about what song I should sing, Jason walked into the pen with a rope. He called softly to his calf. "Here, Army. Come here, boy." When the calf came to him, he dropped the rope over his head and started walking him around the pen.

The calf followed him wherever he went. It was really cool to watch. Meanwhile, Annabelle was looking at my hand, which I'd stretched out to her again. I was afraid she'd bite my fingers, but it was worth a try if I could get her to trust me. "I won't hurt you, Annabelle," I told her in the softest voice I could manage. "We're going to be best friends. I can't wait to take you to the Bradley 4-H Fair. It's going to be the best fair ever! And maybe we'll even win a prize!"

Suddenly I thought of the perfect song to sing to her. It was from *Grease*, which our school had put on a few months ago. I'd played Frenchy, so I didn't get to sing any of the really slow romantic songs. But there was a great song that said exactly how I felt about Annabelle. I was sure it would make her feel closer to me.

I started to sing "Hopelessly Devoted to You." It wasn't easy to sing in the very early morning with no piano or anything to keep me in tune. And I'm not exactly the most in-tune person, anyway. But I sang as loudly as I could to make up for it.

I was really getting into it, but when I looked into the pen, I had the feeling it wasn't the best idea I'd ever had. Annabelle had backed far away from me, into the middle of the pen, and Army, Jason's calf, had stopped following Jason and was tugging so hard on his rope that Jason almost fell backward. I decided it might be a good idea to stop.

Jason was staring at me with the oddest look on his face. I thought I'd try to reassure him. "I was just trying out a theory I had," I explained. "About treating calves like plants. I thought Annabelle might like some music in the morning."

Jason started to laugh. "Sabrina, that noise you're making isn't what I'd call music. I mean, you haven't been exactly on key, and you might try singing a little softer."

I could tell my efforts at creative calf-raising were not appreciated. I knew we had to hurry if we were going to get to school on time, so I wouldn't have a chance to practice any of my other ideas. But that was okay. While I was in school, I could still be working on Project Annabelle. I'd just have to take a different approach, that's all.

Chapter Three

"Sabrina Wells!" I had this awful feeling that Ms. Staats, my English teacher, had been calling my name for some time. Slowly I raised my head and looked at her.

"Well, finally," Ms. Staats said sarcastically. "I was beginning to wonder whether you were having an out-of-body experience."

Everyone around me giggled, and I could feel myself starting to blush. In a split second I knew I was totally red from my scalp to my toes. I'll bet even Ms. Staats noticed.

She must have, because her voice sounded a lot gentler when she said to me, "We're talking about the difference between adjectives and adverbs. Can you explain it?"

Usually I like English class. Today, though, it seemed like I was only thinking about one thing. Well, two things, actually. The first was Annabelle herself and how terrific she was, and the second was winning the ribbon at the 4-H Fair. To tell you the truth, I was just as excited about Annabelle as I was about winning the ribbon!

I tried to concentrate on Ms. Staats's question. She was giving me another chance, so I thought for a minute and said, "Well, they both describe things."

"That's right," Ms. Staats said. "But what's the difference between them?"

My mind was a total blank. I took a wild stab at it. "Well . . . adjectives are positive and adverbs are negative?"

"Sabrina!" By the sharp tone of Ms. Staats's voice, I could tell my guess was not brilliant. I gave up. I had a lot on my mind. How was I going to train Annabelle in time for the fair?

As I was walking to my locker to put my books away before lunch, I wondered when Annabelle's birthday was. Maybe I could check out her horoscope. If people are ruled by the stars, why shouldn't calves be?

Katie was already working our locker combination when I got there. "How'd it go with your calf this morning?" she asked.

"Well," I said, "I've got a great name for her.

I've named her Annabelle."

"Annabelle," Katie murmured. "That's pretty, Sabs. Are you guys getting to be friends?"

"We've started," I said, dropping my English book into the locker. "This morning we were even singing together and everything. Although I don't think she liked my singing too much."

Katie giggled. "You and your calf were singing together? That's a scream!"

I grinned at her. Katie's the best. On the way to the cafeteria, I told her what had happened that morning.

"I'm not sure I can handle it," I finally said as we got to the cafeteria. "I feel like I don't know what to do with her."

"But you just started, Sabs," Katie encouraged me. "It'll take a while to get used to working with her."

I shook my head. "No," I said unhappily. "I want so much for Annabelle to like me, but nothing I try seems to work on her."

Katie thought about this as we stood on line waiting for food. "Well, why not try another way?" she said finally.

"Like what?" I asked.

Katie grinned at me. "How about looking in

the library? Remember what you said yesterday about farming scientifically?" she asked. "I'll bet there are some good books about raising farm animals."

"That's a great idea, Katie!" I cried. "There's no way I can lose with Annabelle once I learn the scientific way of raising a calf!"

I was so excited about Katie's idea that I ate my lunch really quickly and hurried over to the library.

The library was pretty quiet, since everybody else was either in class or at lunch. Good, that meant I'd have the shelves all to myself.

I went over to the card catalog. Luckily, I remembered that you could look up books by subject as well as by title or author. That was good, because I wouldn't have known a single title or author to look up.

I saw Ms. Reed, the librarian, headed my way, so I got busy with the "F" file. "Can I help you find something?" she asked pleasantly.

"I'm okay," I told her. "I've just gotten a calf to raise, and I want to learn all about how to feed and train her."

"Well, then," Ms. Reed said, "you'll probably want to look under 'Animal Husbandry.'"

"Oh, no," I said. "Annabelle's a single calf. She hasn't got a husband. She hasn't got any family except me."

Ms. Reed laughed. "'Husbandry' just means farming," she explained.

"Oh," I said, feeling a little relieved. I closed the "F" drawer and reached for the "A."

I saw the phone on the librarian's desk light up. Ms. Reed noticed it, too. "Sorry, I'd better go," she said. "If you need any help, let me know."

"I will," I told her. Then I got busy looking up the "Animal Husbandry" cards. There were several of them, but most didn't sound like they'd help me at all. There were books on animal medicine, farm buildings, even on training and caring for horses. Randy would probably have loved that one. I didn't think it would help me with a calf, though.

Finally I found a card that sounded just right: *From Calf to Cow: Dairy Farming.* Perfect! The card said that it covered subjects like training calves, feeding and weighing them, and then stuff like selling them, which I wasn't really interested in.

Quickly I copied down the title and the

number from the card and closed the drawer. I'd have to hurry if I was going to find the book and check it out before my next class. I set off to find the book.

Suddenly I heard someone whispering my name. "Hey, Sabrina!" I looked up. Who that I knew would be in the library at this time of the day?

It was Nick. I was really surprised. "What are you doing here?" I asked him.

Nick turned bright red and mumbled something under his breath that I couldn't hear.

"What?" I asked.

"I'm . . . uh . . . checking out a book," he said, looking down at the carpet.

I looked at the book in his hand. It was a gardening book. I thought I'd seen it on the display racks in front. "Is that for a class?" I asked.

Quickly Nick put the book behind his back. "What're *you* doing here?" he asked.

That reminded me — I had to get that book or I'd be late for my next class. At the same time, I remembered how Nick had teased me at Jason's birthday party. I didn't want him making jokes about my ability to raise Annabelle. I started off toward the stacks again.

"Um . . . it's some research I'm doing," I said, trying to sound very businesslike. "For a project."

"What kind of project?" Nick asked. I noticed he was keeping up with me. I wondered whether he was going to come with me while I looked for the book.

"Nothing very important," I said, walking a little faster. Nick walked a little faster, too.

Finally I got to the farming section. Nick looked at the books and then at me. Now I could feel myself blushing. "Research project?" he asked.

"That's right," I answered, hunting on the shelves for *From Calf to Cow*. I checked the number on the piece of paper in my hand, keeping my face turned away from Nick.

"I guess this means your creative methods aren't working very well, huh?" Nick asked, grinning at me. "Jason told me all about how you were singing to your calf this morning. I heard you scared the cows."

I wouldn't give him the satisfaction of admitting it. In fact, I considered telling him once and for all to stop making fun of me. Just then, though, I spotted *From Calf to Cow* on the shelf. I grabbed it and started for the checkout desk.

"Hey, Sabrina!" Nick called after me in a loud whisper. I turned around. He was grinning at me. "Hope the book helps," he said.

That afternoon Jason's father picked us up in his truck to take us to the farm. Nick came, too. I had forgotten that he was supposed to bike home with me. I tried to read the book on the way and ignore Jason and Nick. I figured I could get a head start on my training with Annabelle. After a while, though, I gave up. It's hard enough not getting carsick while bouncing around in a truck; reading at the same time is impossible.

Luckily, Annabelle seemed a lot happier to see me than she had been that morning. I got busy right away, filling a new bucket with water for the trough and checking her grain supply. She'd eaten most of her grain, so I filled her up again. I was very proud that I'd remembered everything Jason had done in the morning. All I had to do now, I figured, was give her some fresh hay. Then I could get busy getting to know her better and training her for the fair.

As I was carrying fresh hay out to the pen, I

heard Jason laughing. When I looked up, I saw him talking to Nick, who grinned and waved when he saw me.

Oh, no! I didn't want to train Annabelle with Nick watching me. He'd be sure to make some crack. I really wanted to get down to working hard, and I didn't want anyone making fun of me.

"Hey, Sabrina," Jason called. "Nick's going to help us with the training. This should really be fun."

"Yeah, great," I said, gritting my teeth. Obviously Nick intended to hang out all afternoon, watching and laughing at my mistakes. But why would he waste his time if he thought I was so dumb? Didn't he have something better to do?

Well, I'd show him. While I was waiting for Annabelle to finish eating, I skimmed through the book, checking out the sections on training a calf. The book said that first-time trainers usually had to overcome their own fear of the animal, before they could really communicate with the calf.

I thought about that for a minute. I had been a little frightened of Annabelle that morning. Maybe that was why she had backed away from me. The book mentioned that touching the calf was important in establishing communication and suggested scratching it behind its ears.

That sounded pretty good. While Annabelle was chomping on her grain, I reached out to stroke her head. She raised her head right away and looked at me, but I didn't get the feeling that she was mad. She just seemed to wonder what was going on.

"Hi, Annabelle," I said in my softest tone. "How's everything?" Reaching out, I scratched her behind the ears.

It worked! In a second Annabelle nuzzled her head against my hand, just the way my dog, Cinnamon, does when you scratch her in the same place. Annabelle was definitely showing me that she liked it. I was on my way to being friends with her at last!

"That's really good," Jason told me as he came up to the pen. "She's starting to trust you."

"Yeah, well, she doesn't know Sabrina very well," Nick cracked. "Give her a little time."

I kept scratching Annabelle behind the ears,

ignoring everything Nick said. She went right back to her grain, rubbing her head against me while she ate. I tried to read up on calf-training as fast as I could. I wanted to be all set to teach Annabelle once dinner was over.

Unfortunately, I was getting a little flustered with Nick standing close by. I could hardly concentrate on what I was reading. When Annabelle looked up from her grain, I quickly went into the pen.

"Sabrina," Jason called.

"In a minute, Jason," I called back. Couldn't he see I was busy working with my calf?

"Sabrina," Jason called again. This time he sounded impatient. I looked over. He held up a rope. "You can't lead her without a halter, remember? That should be in the book, too."

It was. I just hadn't been able to concentrate very well. "Thanks," I told him, and slung the halter over my shoulder. I went straight for Annabelle, walking slowly and softly, talking to her, reaching out my hand to scratch her behind the ears again. "Come on, Annabelle," I told her. "We're going to go for a little walk now, just as soon as I get this halter on you. Don't worry about a thing. Wearing a halter is very chic for calves. You're going to look great."

As soon as she felt my hand, she stood very still. I was able to slip the halter right over her head. She let me fasten the rope and everything. It took me a few tries to figure out how it worked, but I just kept right on talking to her while I struggled. "That's great, Annabelle. You look really good with this halter around your neck. You look like a real prizewinner right now." I figured it couldn't hurt to build up her confidence.

Finally I got the halter fastened and started to walk around the pen. Annabelle didn't quite seem to get it. She wasn't budging. "Come on, Annabelle," I told her. "We're going to walk now. Let's go, Annabelle. Walk right behind me." But she just stood there.

I went over and scratched her behind the ears again. She seemed to love that, because she rubbed her head against me. But when I tried to get her to walk around, she didn't move.

To make matters worse, Nick was snickering at me as I tried to coax Annabelle to lead.

"Nice going, Sabs," he called. "She looks

like she's ready to move anytime now. Like Christmas!"

"That's right," Jason added. "If she keeps standing there, you'll be able to plant something around her!"

I was mad now. Jason was really nice when we were alone together, but it seemed whenever he got together with Nick, they egged each other on.

I tried for a long time, but Annabelle didn't take a single step. I could feel tears welling up in my eyes. If she was going to be stubborn, how would I ever get her trained in time for the fair? What was worse, Nick kept up a steady stream of insults. "Too bad you're not a boy, Sabs. Boys do a lot better with farm animals than girls. But it's not your fault. For a girl, you're still doing pretty rotten!" He thought he was a riot.

Finally Jason came into the pen and took the halter from me. He could see I was really down, and he didn't make any nasty cracks. "Time to milk the cows," he said quietly. "Would you like to milk Alma, Sabs?"

I put my head down and just nodded so he wouldn't see the tears in my eyes.

I found Alma and got right to work milking her just the way Jason had shown me that morning. "You're doing great, Sabrina," he said after a while. "You've got a great touch with Alma."

"Tell that to Annabelle," I said unhappily. "And to Nick," I added.

Jason looked at me for a second, not saying anything. Then he turned and walked away. When he came back, he had Annabelle with him. Together, they watched me milk Alma until the pail was full. Annabelle even started pulling on my sweater. When I was finished, I gave the pail to Jason.

"Take her back to the pen," he said, handing me Annabelle's rope. I expected her to stand there as stubbornly as before, but as soon as I started toward the pen, Annabelle followed very happily. She didn't tug at the rope or dig in her heels or anything. I got her into the pen next to Army in record time. It really surprised me. Maybe she figured if I could handle a full-grown cow, she could trust me, too. Whatever it was, it made me feel better.

Nick saw me lead Annabelle out of the barn. I thought he'd make some crack, but he didn't say a word. I took off the halter, petted Annabelle, and said good night to her, then left the pen. Nick was looking at me as I shut the gate, but when I glanced back at him, he turned away quickly.

"See?" Jason said as he came up to the pen. "She's getting used to you. You're doing great with her."

"Thanks, Jason," I said. "I'll see you tomorrow morning, bright and early."

I stuck *From Calf to Cow* into my backpack, grabbed my bike, and started down the driveway. Behind me I heard Nick saying good-bye to Jason and hurrying after me. I knew that we were supposed to be riding home together, but I didn't really want to be teased anymore.

It was funny, though. Nick wasn't talking to me. It was getting dark and cold and the wind was blowing hard. By the time we were halfway home, Nick hadn't made a single crack. In fact, he didn't say a single word.

I thought maybe I should say something. I didn't want him to make fun of me, so I tried to think of something neutral. "Are you enjoying that gardening book?" I asked.

Nick turned red and gave me the meanest

look I had ever seen from him. "That's really rude," he said angrily. "Considering the way you handled Annabelle today, I wouldn't say you were exactly the expert of the world on the natural world."

I was shocked. I couldn't believe Nick could get that mad at me, especially when I hadn't even said anything mean. We didn't say anything at all for the rest of the ride home.

I had a feeling I'd gone too far, but I didn't even know how or with what. Why was he so mean to me all of a sudden?

Chapter Four

(Sabrina calls Katie.)

KATIE: Campbell and Beauvais residence.

SABRINA: Katie? It's Sabs.

KATIE: Sabs! Hi! How's it going with Annabelle?

SABRINA: Well, right now, Annabelle's not my problem. Nick's my problem.

KATIE: Nick? Why is Nick a problem?

SABRINA: Katie, you won't believe it, but I think he hates me.

KATIE: Sabrina Wells! Nick does not hate you!

SABRINA: That's what you think. Remember how at Jason's party he was making those really mean remarks about girls doing farm work? He keeps acting like he thinks I'm some kind of bingo head or something. You should have seen him

44

today. He watched me feeding Annabelle and made all these comments about girls not being as good as boys. Then, after I finally got Annabelle to walk with me, he didn't say a word.

KATIE: Nothing?

SABRINA: Honestly, Katie. Not a single word. When I tried to talk to him about something that happened in the library today —

KATIE: You saw him in the library?

SABRINA: Yes, when I was checking out that book on calves. Didn't I tell you?

KATIE: No. What happened?

SABRINA: Well, the library was really quiet at lunchtime. Then, all of a sudden, Nick said hi to me. He had some gardening book with him. He said he was checking it out.

KATIE: A gardening book? Why would Nick want a gardening book?

SABRINA: That's what I wondered. But I didn't say anything about it till we were riding our bikes home. I wasn't putting him down or anything, Katie. He just wasn't talking to me at all, and I was trying to think of something to say, so I asked him how he liked his gardening book. He got really upset.

KATIE: Oh, no!

SABRINA: What?

KATIE: Don't you see, Sabs? He really likes you!

SABRINA: Why do you think he likes me?

KATIE: It's obvious. He probably followed you into the library, but he couldn't think of an excuse for being there, so he grabbed the first book he saw. That's why he was so embarrassed about it.

SABRINA: Yeah? And what about this afternoon? If he likes me so much, why wouldn't he talk to me on the way home?

KATIE: You know what? I bet he's really impressed with what you're doing with Annabelle.

SABRINA: Katie! Are you nuts? He thinks my training Annabelle is the dumbest idea of the year.

KATIE: No, listen, Sabs. When he saw
            how well you did with Annabelle,
            he couldn't really tease you about
            not being good at farm work. But
            he also couldn't admit that he was
            wrong. So he didn't say anything
            at all. I bet he really wanted to tell
            you you were doing great.

SABRINA: Katie, this sounds like something
            out of a movie or something. Real
            boys don't go around being too
            choked up to say anything.

KATIE: Come on, Sabs, you know Nick's
            always liked you. Remember the
            homecoming dance at the begin-
            ning of the year? When he asked
            you to go and then refused to take
            you at the last minute because he
            thought you liked another guy?

SABRINA: Yeah . . .

KATIE: It's sort of the same thing now.
            Nick just can't admit how he feels
            about you. He probably thinks
            you'd laugh at him. Or maybe
            he's afraid his friends would
            laugh at him. But the reason he's

hanging around you is because he likes you. I'm sure of that.

SABRINA: So what do I do?

KATIE: I don't know.

SABRINA: Maybe I should talk to Allison and see what she thinks.

KATIE: That's a good idea. Al can always think of something.

SABRINA: I'll call her. Thanks for everything, Katie.

KATIE: Good luck, Sabs. Keep me posted.

(*Sabrina calls Allison.*)

ALLISON: Hello, Allison Cloud speaking.

SABRINA: Al, it's Sabs.

ALLISON: Oh, Sabrina, hi!

SABRINA: Al, I've got a real problem. Katie thought you might have an idea.

ALLISON: What is it?

SABRINA: It's Nick. He was hanging around this afternoon while I was working with Annabelle. He's been teasing me a lot lately and really hurting my feelings. But Katie says it's because he really likes me and doesn't know how to let me

	know it.
ALLISON:	I think Katie's right, Sabs. He really does like you.
SABRINA:	So what do I do now?
ALLISON:	Well, it depends on what you want.
SABRINA:	What do you mean?
ALLISON:	I mean, do you like Nick, too? I mean, *like* like? Or do you just think of him as a friend?
SABRINA:	Gee, I don't know. I guess . . . I think I just want him to treat me nicer. I don't want him to keep making fun of me. I mean, he used to be so nice.
ALLISON:	Okay. Then you have to prove to him that you're really capable with Annabelle. Show him he has to respect you.
SABRINA:	You mean so he can't make fun of me anymore?
ALLISON:	Exactly. Don't give him a chance to say anything mean about you. If you train Annabelle well, there's no way he can make fun of you. He won't have anything to

	pick on.
SABRINA:	But how will I prove to him that I've done a great job with Annabelle?
ALLISON:	Hmm, I don't know. Maybe you should talk to Randy.
SABRINA:	I will. Randy always knows the right way to stop somebody from picking on you. I'll call her right now. Thanks, Allison.
ALLISON:	Anytime, Sabs.

(Sabrina calls Randy.)

RANDY:	Yo! Randy Zak here!
SABRINA:	Randy, it's Sabs.
RANDY:	Hiya. What's happening?
SABRINA:	Listen, I've been talking to Katie and Allison. Nick's been making fun of me because of Annabelle.
RANDY:	Sounds to me like he's got a major crush on you.
SABRINA:	That's what Katie and Al said. They think I should show Nick that I'm so good with Annabelle he can't pick on me anymore. But how do I prove it to him?

RANDY: This is a problem? Please, Sabs. The answer's so obvious.

SABRINA: Well, what is it?

RANDY: The 4-H Fair, of course. If you take a prize at the fair, Nick'll have to respect you, because everybody else will. Doesn't that make total sense?

SABRINA: It really does! Randy, you're a genius!

RANDY: I know.

SABRINA: But do you think I can train Annabelle well enough to take a prize at the fair?

RANDY: Sure you can. If you spend enough time with her, I'll bet you can get Annabelle to do anything you want. I'll bet you win first place. If Nick tries to make fun of you after that, he'll look like a real jerk.

SABRINA: You're right! Then we can go back to being friends.

RANDY: Or maybe something else.

SABRINA: You mean, like boyfriend-girl-friend?

RANDY: Well, it's possible. Anyway, you won't have him hurting your feelings anymore.

SABRINA: That's true. Thanks a million, Randy. I think you've really hit on something!

RANDY: See you in school tomorrow, Sabs. *Ciao.*

SABRINA: You bet!

Chapter Five

With my friends behind me, I really went to work on Annabelle every afternoon that week. I read *From Calf to Cow* cover to cover. It gave me some good advice, and Annabelle did just what the book said she would. Most important, I talked to her all the time, and I was sure she was really getting to like me as a person.

At lunchtime on Friday I loaded up my tray. Usually I try to pick healthy foods, but that day I was starving. I had a big helping of meatloaf with a whole pile of mashed potatoes. I even helped myself to a huge chocolate brownie.

As I walked through the cafeteria, looking for Katie, Al, and Randy, I noticed a lot of posters for the Bradley 4-H Fair. It seemed like everybody I talked to was getting involved with some kind of exhibit or competition. In fact, a lot of people couldn't talk about anything else.

"Over here!" I heard Randy yell. She waved an arm at me. It was hard to miss Randy. She was wearing this super black lace shirt, plus a dozen black bangle bracelets. Katie and Allison were already sitting at her table. I hurried over.

"How's it going with Annabelle?" Katie asked as I started eating.

"Really well," I told her. "We're starting to work together — it's great!"

Then I realized something. I was the only one of our group who was participating in the fair! It didn't seem right.

"Hey, guys," I began, "how come you're not doing something for the fair? I don't want to be the only one trying for a prize."

"You mean we should all raise calves?" Randy said with a laugh.

"No, not raise calves," I said. "But the fair has lots of other events. We should all enter at least one. Come on, it would be fun."

"What do you think we should do?" Allison asked. I knew Al would be tough to convince. She's a little shy, and I knew she wouldn't want to get up in front of strangers and show off. At the same time I knew she'd be missing something if she didn't get involved. It seemed like every kid at Bradley was doing something. I didn't want my friends to be left out.

Randy pointed her fork at Katie. "*You* should do that quilting thing," she told Katie. "I love the quilt you've been making."

Katie blushed. It was true — she has a real talent for making quilting squares. She's very patient and spends a lot of time sewing them, so every stitch is just right. It must be the Virgo in her. She's a real perfectionist. "*Is* there a quilting contest?" she asked.

"Sure there is!" I told her. "Don't you remember, Mr. Hansen read that announcement in homeroom about all the events? The top twelve blocks will get sewn into the final quilt, which will be hung up in the lobby. It would be great for you, Katie! Come on!"

Katie blushed. "Well, all right," she said. "I guess it would be kind of fun."

"Great!" I said excitedly. "What're you going to do, Randy?"

Randy looked a little skeptical. "I don't know, Sabs. I mean, 4-H is kind of country time, isn't it? We didn't have a 4-H club at my old school in New York."

"So what? You could pick something wild

and do that. Come on, Randy," I pleaded.

"You could make a funky egg for the egg contest," Katie suggested.

Randy shook her head. "I just can't get into painting eggs, guys. It's not me."

"How about the horse-grooming competition?" Allison asked. "You love horses."

Randy looked gloomy. "But I don't have a horse here," she pointed out. "I don't have any tack, either. It's hard to groom a horse if you haven't got a horse or a horse kit to work with."

I could see she was right. This was going to be tough. Randy would never agree to enter a knitting contest, and she'd hate the idea of growing vegetables, even if she had the time to do it. We'd have to find something unusual for her to do.

I was thinking so hard about Randy's event that I didn't even notice we had company until I heard an ultrasweet voice croon, "Well, hi, Sabrina. I hear you're entering the 4-H Fair, too."

I didn't have to look up to know who it was. It couldn't have been anybody but Stacy the Great. Sure enough, there she was, in this short yellow skirt with what looked like a thousand pleats in it, a silky yellow shirt that matched it perfectly, and yellow heels. Sometimes I think Stacy has heels in every color. I wish I could wear them, too, but my mom says it could hurt my legs and back unless I wait until I'm fully grown.

Stacy gave me this sickening smile when I looked up at her. "I'm entering the dairy competition," I told her. I just knew she'd have something snide to say.

Sure enough, Stacy tried to look surprised. "Dairy? You mean a calf? Really, Sabrina. Why not try something a little more feminine?"

"Like what?" I asked, feeling angry. First Nick made fun of me for raising Annabelle. Now it was Stacy. I was definitely getting tired of it.

"Like the pie contest. It's cherry pie this year, and I've got a recipe that nobody can beat," Stacy said. As she smiled at me again, her clones, Laurel Spencer, B. Z. Latimer, and Eva Malone, came up behind her. "I'm telling them about my cherry pie," Stacy told her friends. "Isn't it the greatest?"

"It's delicious," Laurel said.

"I've never tasted anything better," Eva

chimed in.

"Really. It's to die for," B.Z. added.

Randy glared at Stacy. "Too bad, Stacy. I hate seeing you lose the contest."

"Oh? How could I possibly lose?" Stacy asked, still in that sweet voice. I was getting cavities just listening to her.

"Because," Randy said in an equally sweet voice, "it happens that Bradley's all-time champion cherry-pie baker is sitting right here."

I stared at Randy. It's true that she could cook up a storm, but it wasn't like her to brag. I was really surprised she'd say something like that. I was even more surprised when she went on. "You haven't *lived* until you've tasted Allison's cherry pie."

I could tell Allison was even more shocked than I was. She opened her mouth to say something but closed it again, real fast. Randy put her hand on Allison's shoulder. "Of course, Al doesn't go around bragging like you do, Stacy," she went on. "In fact, she wasn't even going to enter, because her pie's so great, nobody else's comes even close. But *I* think she should enter — just to blow you out of the water. What do you say, Al?"

We were all frozen in our seats. I could tell Stacy and her clones were shocked, too. But Stacy didn't wait for Allison to answer. She just flipped her blond hair over her shoulder and turned away. "We'll see at the fair," she hissed at Randy.

"We sure will," Randy replied calmly. "Sorry you'll have to be so humiliated. But Al will save you a piece of her pie for after the contest. So you can taste a real winner."

Stacy marched away, her clones right behind her. We all burst out laughing. "Randy, that was brilliant!" Katie exclaimed. "Stacy'll hate it if Al's pie beats hers out."

"I didn't even know you could make a cherry pie, Al," I said. "What else can you bake?"

Allison didn't look very well. She shook her head, and her voice was very low. "That's just it. I can't bake anything at all."

"*What?*" I asked. Either I wasn't hearing right, or we were in a lot of trouble. "You mean you can't bake cherry pie, either?"

Allison shook her head miserably. "I don't even eat cherry pie," she moaned. "Randy, how could you tell Stacy I was a champion baker?"

"Hey, no problem, Al," Randy insisted.

"Two lessons with me and you'll be a four-star baker. I love to cook. Come on, trust me. We can work on it at my house after school."

I felt like I should offer to help Allison, too. After all, it was my idea in the first place that everybody get involved in the fair. "I'll taste your pies when you bake them," I volunteered. "That way, I can give you pointers on what's working and what isn't."

"You also get to eat a lot of cherry pie," Randy pointed out.

"What's wrong with that?" I asked. "It'll keep up my strength for working with Annabelle."

"She's right," Katie said with a laugh. "We'll all be helping each other."

For the first time since Stacy left, Allison smiled. "I guess that means I'll have to help Randy come up with an event she can enter at the fair," she said.

"It's got to be something cool," Randy insisted. "I'm not doing anything dorky. I've got an image to maintain, you know."

We knew. Whatever Randy ended up doing at the fair was sure to be the next new, hip thing. It was going to be interesting figuring out just what that would be!

Chapter Six

It was late afternoon by the time I finished working with Annabelle and my dad came and dropped me off at Randy's house. We were all having a sleepover there so we could help Allison bake her pie.

Randy and her mother live in this beautiful restored barn. Her mother, who always asks us to call her by her first name, Olivia, is an artist, and she has made the barn look great. Randy's bedroom is in the loft, and Olivia has set Chinese screens around her own bedroom on the main floor. It is really cool.

When I got there, Randy and Allison were already wearing aprons and watching the kitchen timer. Katie was setting four places at the table. "We put the pie in almost an hour ago," Randy told me. "It'll be ready to taste any minute."

"Great," I replied. "I'm starving." Usually after school we head to Fitzie's for a soda. Fitzie's is where everybody at Bradley hangs out. But lately, because of Annabelle, I didn't have time to go to Fitzie's. I was definitely in the mood for something sweet.

The timer buzzed suddenly. "Fresh hot pie!" I yelled. "I can't wait!"

"Okay, Al, take the pie out," Randy instructed. She watched as Allison carefully used heavy potholders to open the oven door and lift the pie out. It looked a little different from most pies, and I tried to figure out why.

As Allison set the pie on a wire rack to cool, I realized the top looked just a little browner than other pie crusts. Well, that was okay. Pie crust tastes good when it's flaky.

"We have to wait fifteen minutes or so for the pie to cool," Randy explained. While we were waiting, she got sodas from the refrigerator and poured them into tall glasses. "Al did the whole thing herself," Randy went on. "I didn't even look at her recipe."

"I wanted to get used to doing it on my own, for the contest," Allison explained.

Katie nodded. "That's a good idea. That

way, you won't be afraid of doing it yourself."

"Exactly," Allison answered. "I want to be prepared."

I leaned over the hot pie and took a deep breath. It smelled a little funny, but I figured that had to be because it was still hot from the oven. When it cooled down, I knew it would be delicious. Allison was so good at her schoolwork and stuff that she was probably a naturally talented baker, too.

We sat sipping our sodas and eyeing the pie. "Any ideas about what you're going to do, Randy?" Katie asked.

Randy shook her head. "Al's been trying to convince me I should enter a weaving contest, but I can't see it. Weaving's just not for me." She glanced at her watch. "Okay, let's try it."

Randy carefully cut slices of the pie. I got the first slice, which was just a tiny bit runny. Allison looked nervous. "Don't worry, Al," I assured her. "I'm sure it's yummy."

"I hope so," Allison answered softly. "I borrowed the recipe from my mother's old cookbook. I hope it turned out all right."

She watched me nervously as I cut off a piece and put it in my mouth. Oh, no! I grabbed my soda and drank it down as fast as I could. "How is it?" Allison asked quickly.

"Oh, uh, it's . . . *different* from any cherry pie I've ever had," I said, trying to be tactful. It was the worst pie I'd ever eaten in my whole life! The cherries tasted like they'd been burned, and the pie crust wasn't just flaky, it tasted like cardboard. The whole thing had a definite charcoal taste. It was awful.

Katie tasted hers next. She swallowed her first bite, then looked up at Allison, who looked hopefully back at her. "This is . . . a really good first try, Allison," she managed to say.

"Really?" Allison asked.

"Oh, yes," Katie said. "You can't expect to get the entire thing right on the first try. This is a . . . really interesting first pie."

Now Randy tried hers. Her eyes got so wide, I thought they were going to pop right out. "What is it, Randy?" Allison asked anxiously.

Randy put down her fork. "Al, we've got some major problems here. Come on, taste it."

We all waited silently while Allison took a bite. Her eyes got wide, too. "Oh, no. This is terrible." She groaned. When she said that, we all burst out laughing, and Allison was laughing as hard as the rest of us.

"What did you mix in with the cherries?" I asked curiously. "It tastes like, uh —"

"I know what you mean," Katie agreed. "It tastes a little like sour cream."

Allison blushed. "In my mother's recipe, you're supposed to mix in a little heavy cream, but you're supposed to have the cream at room temperature. I figured if I did that, the cream would go sour, so I put in sour cream instead."

"It's a lethal weapon!" Randy said, pointing to her piece. "If we feed this to Stacy, she might not live to compete in the pie contest!"

Allison's smile vanished. "But what am I going to do?" she asked. "After what you said in the cafeteria, Stacy's going to expect me to make a really good pie."

"Don't worry," Randy told her. "This is a start. You got the right amount of cherries in here, and you rolled the pie crust just the right way. You've got a week to figure it out."

"Maybe you should think about baking it at the right temperature next time," Katie suggested. "This tastes a little . . . burned."

"That's right," I agreed. "Maybe the oven

was too hot."

"What temperature did you set the oven at?" Randy asked.

Allison looked dazed. "I didn't even look," she admitted. "I just turned on the oven to 'bake' and figured it was set."

I couldn't help it. I burst out laughing again, and everybody else followed. Soon, though, Allison was writing down everyone's suggestions for improving the pie.

"Next pie tomorrow," Allison said cheerfully when she'd written down all our ideas.

"Maybe we should enter this one in the contest and put Stacy's name on it." Randy laughed. We all laughed. Somehow, with everyone now involved in the fair, it was becoming even more fun.

I began to worry about Randy, though. None of our ideas seemed to interest her. I thought she should have entered the pie contest herself, but she insisted that baking was just fun for her. She didn't want to try for any prizes.

She was having a lot of fun teaching Allison to bake, though. Every day Allison brought a new pie in to school for us to taste. She really began to get the hang of it. After that first awful pie, she'd started to learn how to pick the right kind of cherries, how to mix them, and how to make a good pie crust. In fact, she started doing some wild experiments, trying to come up with the ultimate cherry-pie recipe.

By Wednesday I realized I was beginning to hate cherry pie. In fact, I was considering never eating cherry pie again when the 4-H Fair was over. I didn't like the idea of eating more pie at lunch, but then I realized I was doing it for Allison. You have to make certain sacrifices for a friend.

Randy had her Walkman on, and the music was blaring so loudly that we could all hear it. It was a rap song, and Randy was rapping right along with the lead singer. She sounded pretty good, too. It was almost too bad she was already the drummer in the group Iron Wombat. I was sure she could also be lead singer of a rap group if she ever wanted to be.

Randy started to change the tape in her Walkman. "You've got to hear this one, guys, it's really righteous!"

Allison stared at Randy like a light had suddenly come on. "Randy, that's it!" she cried.

"What?" Randy asked, looking up.

"The 4-H Fair — I know the perfect thing for you to do!" Allison exclaimed.

"What?" Randy asked. She was probably getting a little tired of all our suggestions. Every time we mentioned something, she told us it was too dorky or uncool or not for her. We'd thought of all kinds of things, but she didn't like any of them. I was beginning to wonder whether we'd find something for her at all.

"What's your idea, Al?" Katie asked.

Allison explained her idea to us.

Randy grinned when she finished. "I love it, Al!" she exclaimed. "That sounds absolutely awesome!"

Katie grinned, too. "That's the best idea for the fair I've heard yet," she said. "You're a genius, Allison."

Allison blushed. "It seemed to make a lot of sense," she said.

"It sure does," I agreed. "Between your cherry pie and Randy's event, it looks like our group'll be the hit of the fair!"

Chapter Seven

Suddenly it was time for the fair. Bradley was full of posters and announcements about various events, and everyone at school was talking about the events they were entering.

Jason and I were entering the calves' fitting and showmanship contest with Army and Annabelle. Jason had a lot more experience than I did, and he'd been working with Army longer. I didn't know how to make up for that, and it was really important to me to show Nick that I could win a ribbon in the fair.

Annabelle and I were great friends now, just like I thought we would be. She was always waiting for me when I came to feed her in the morning and after school. She loved it when I stroked her ears and scratched her head.

After she got used to working in the pen, I started singing to her again, very softly, so nobody else could hear. She really seemed to like it, especially when I sang songs from *Grease* and sixties oldies. She particularly liked the Beatles and Petula Clark. I guess she had a weakness for British singers.

Now, instead of telling her to walk or trot or stand still, I sang to her. When I sang a Beatles song, she trotted around the ring. When I sang "Summer Nights" from *Grease*, she stood still, and when she heard Petula Clark's "Downtown," she walked at a nice pace right behind me. I had a feeling that my musical relationship with Annabelle would be the deciding factor in the 4-H contest.

The other important part of the contest was Annabelle's grooming. The 4-H Fair judges called it "fitting" a calf, but they meant how clean it was and how well it was clipped and brushed and taken care of. I had to make sure Annabelle looked good to them.

Jason let me use a hose and one of the farm's washracks for Annabelle's baths. I always checked that the water was nice and warm for her. I didn't want her either freezing or burning. I also used special soap to wash her as clean as possible. Since she was black and white, the yellow hay stains she got on her really showed. I knew the judges would want to see a perfectly scrubbed Annabelle, so I washed her from top to bottom every other day. Jason laughed at me. He told me I didn't have to wash her that often, but I needed to practice my washrack technique. Annabelle didn't seem to mind. While she was in the washrack, I sang to her. Once in a while she even tossed her head a little, like she was dancing to the beat. She was definitely a calf with rhythm.

On the day before the fair, Allison, Katie, Randy, and I rode out to Jason's farm on our bikes. Katie had a big picnic basket strapped to hers. It was a beautiful Saturday morning, and we were going to have a picnic. I wanted to show them how well I worked with Annabelle, and they were going to help me bathe and groom her for the contest. Afterward, we'd have the picnic. Naturally, Allison had baked a cherry pie for dessert.

Randy had bragged all over school that Allison's pie would win the blue ribbon, and Jason kept hinting about cherry pie all the time, so we invited him on our picnic, too.

Randy loved hearing about how I was training Annabelle with music. "What a fantastic idea, Sabs," she exclaimed as we pedaled along. "A rock 'n' roll calf!"

I didn't tell Randy that Annabelle didn't have a wide selection of favorites. Randy was so interested in new, hip music that she might have been disappointed if she knew that my calf only trotted if I sang "I Want to Hold Your Hand."

"I'll bet Nick's really impressed," Katie said, breaking into my thoughts. "Has he seen you with Annabelle lately?"

"No," I told her, "not at all." Actually, I hadn't seen Nick much since the day we rode our bikes home together and I asked him about the gardening book. He didn't even come by the house to see Sam anymore. When he and Sam wanted to shoot hoops, Sam always went to his house now.

I felt really bad about that. Nick had always been great to me, until I started working with Annabelle. I had thought a lot about all the times he'd stuck up for me when Sam teased me and about the time we slow-danced together at the homecoming dance last fall. Now it seemed like such a long time ago. "Maybe he really does hate me," I blurted out.

"Who hates you? Nick?" Allison asked.

I nodded. "I'm sure of it," I said. "He's probably so mad at me for asking him about the gardening book that he'll never want to talk to me again."

"I don't think so, Sabs," Katie said seriously. "I have a feeling he just doesn't know how to show you that he likes you."

"That's right," Randy chimed in. "Let's face it, boys are not always what you'd call mature. There were times my friend Sheck in New York did some really dumb things! Mostly, it's because they don't want anyone to know they've got these feelings. I think they're afraid someone will make fun of them."

"Well, I wouldn't make fun of Nick's feelings about me!" I said hotly. "He should know better than that!"

"But what about his friends?" Allison pointed out. "Think about how Sam would tease him if he knew Nick really liked you."

Allison had a point. Sam was not the kindest person in the world, especially when he saw a chance to tease somebody. I, of all people, should know that.

So if Nick was afraid of what Sam would say to him, it would make sense that he'd try to act really cool around me. That way, nobody would make fun of him. Still, if he liked me, you'd think he'd want to let *me* know it.

I saw the McKee farm straight ahead and decided not to think about Nick at all for the rest of the day. I had too much to do getting Annabelle ready for the fair, I told myself.

As we rode into the driveway, I looked over and saw a shiny blue bike leaning against the gate. *Nick's bike!* Oh, no!

"What's the matter, Sabs?" Allison asked. "You look kind of funny."

"That's Nick's bike," I said, pointing at the blue bike.

"That means he's here," Katie said.

"Good!" said Randy.

"Good? What do you mean, 'good'?" I asked. "He's the last person I want to see."

Randy got off her bike and leaned it against the gate, next to Nick's. "Don't be a bingo head, Sabs," she said. "Don't you see? This is your chance to show Nick just how much you've done with Annabelle. I'll bet he'll be so impressed, you two will make up right here!"

That made me feel a little better. It was true that Nick hadn't seen me since I'd really gotten into Annabelle's training. Maybe he would be impressed. Suddenly I felt a lot more confident.

"Okay, guys," I said in my best take-charge tone. "Let's go get 'em!"

We grabbed the picnic basket and headed for the barn. I was kind of surprised that Jason and Nick weren't with Army and Annabelle, but when I looked over at the pen, it was empty. I guessed that the calves were with the other dairy cows. Jason often took them out so they could graze with the others. It was good practice for when they got older, he told me.

"What'll we do now?" Allison asked, seeing that the pen was empty.

I tried to sound confident. "No problem. Come on in the barn. Maybe Alma needs milking. I can show you how to milk a cow."

"Sabrina Wells, champion cow-milker!" Katie giggled. "Here we all thought you were going to be a famous actress!"

I laughed, too. "I've got a lot of talents," I told them. "Just because I can play Juliet doesn't mean I can't also train a calf."

We were all laughing when we walked into

the barn, but I stopped laughing right away.
Nick and Jason were in the barn already, milking Alma!

Actually, Nick was doing the milking, while
Jason stood next to him. Neither of them
noticed us. Jason was too busy telling Nick
what to do, and Nick was trying really hard to
follow directions. It was pretty obvious,
though, that he'd never been close to a cow
before in his whole life!

"Now, lean your head against her," Jason
told Nick.

Nick looked a little nervous about that.
"Can't I just reach under her?" he asked. "Do I
have to lean against her, too?"

"Yeah, you have to get close to her," Jason
said. "It'll be easier for you, and she'll feel better."

I started to giggle. I couldn't help it, Nick
looked so funny and forlorn. Alma stood
patiently, but she didn't look too happy, either.

Suddenly Jason looked up and saw us
standing there. So did Nick. His whole face
flushed this bright pink color when he saw me.
I didn't think until our eyes met that maybe he
was learning how to milk Alma just so he could

impress me!

"Hi, Sabs," Jason said casually, like he taught people how to milk cows every day. "Come to see Annabelle?"

I nodded. "I want Katie and Al and Randy to see me lead her. Besides, we are going to get her bathed and groomed for the fair."

"Well, go ahead," Jason said. "We'll be out in a minute."

That didn't make any sense. "How can I?" I asked. "She and Army must still be with the others in the pasture."

Now Jason looked puzzled. "We didn't send them out to graze today," he said slowly.

We looked at each other for a long moment. "Then where are they?" I asked.

"I don't know," Jason admitted. He stood thinking for a minute. Then, in a flash, he ran out the door.

I followed him, worrying about Annabelle. What could have happened to her?

Jason got to the pen and looked it over. Army and Annabelle were nowhere to be seen.

"What happened to them, Jason?" I cried. "What if somebody stole them? What if . . ."

Jason checked around the outside of the

pen. At the very back he found a hole. It looked like it had been forced from being a small hole to being a much larger one. "What is it?" I gasped.

Jason looked grim. "I guess this hole opened up and the calves pushed at it until it was big enough to walk through. Then they just walked out of the pen."

"But where could they have gone?" I said frantically. I had terrible visions in my mind of Annabelle wandering out to the road and maybe getting hit by a car. It was so awful, I couldn't even think about it.

"Don't worry, Sabs," Jason assured me. "Maybe they just went to join the other cows. We'll find them. Come on."

He led the way to the pasture, which is really beautiful. That's where I'd planned to have our picnic. Right now, though, food was the last thing on my mind. I couldn't think of anything except getting Annabelle back.

I heard a low voice beside me. "Don't worry, Sabs," Nick said quietly. "I'm sure she's all right."

I looked at him. He wasn't making fun of me. I could tell he was as worried about

Annabelle as I was. It made me feel good that Nick was concerned. I began to have a funny, mushy feeling in the pit of my stomach.

I was so anxious about Annabelle that I ran ahead of Jason to the pasture, calling to her. I could see a big herd of cows moving around lazily. Most of them had pretty much the same coloring, which made it tough to look for Annabelle. She was also a lot smaller than the grown cows. She could easily be hiding between two of them and I might not even see her.

Jason waded right into the herd, calling for Army and Annabelle. Nick, Randy, Katie, and Al wandered around the edge of the herd, checking to be sure the cows didn't run off and looking for Army and Annabelle, too. I alternated between squeezing among the cows and running around the outside. Nobody saw any sign of the calves.

"Hey, look, Sabs, it's okay." Jason tried to reassure me. "It means they went off by themselves. I'll bet when we find one of them, we'll find the other, too."

"But where do we look for them?" I cried.

Jason thought about it. "How about the

washracks?" he suggested.

"That's a great idea!" Allison agreed. "If Annabelle spends a lot of time there, she just might have wandered over."

"Maybe she thinks she's going to get a Top-40 bath." Randy giggled.

I tried to laugh, but I was too worried about my calf. I couldn't help thinking that something awful might have happened to her and that I hadn't even been around to prevent it. Suddenly I didn't feel as mature and responsible as I'd felt for the last week. I began to wonder whether it wasn't somehow all my fault.

We hurried over to the washracks. There wasn't an animal in sight. It didn't even look as though Army and Annabelle had been over there. Everything was still stacked in neat piles.

"Well, they weren't here," I said, feeling discouraged.

"Maybe they went into the barn," Nick suggested.

"Good idea," Jason agreed. "Let's go!"

We all hurried after him, but I was beginning to feel hopeless. Nobody had any idea what might have happened to our calves. They could have gone anywhere. Right now Jason was looking everywhere we suggested, but sooner or later we'd all run out of ideas. Then what would happen? Were we supposed to call the police and file a missing calves report?

Alma stood by her milking pail, just as we'd left her. Jason tore through the whole barn, looking into all the stalls. He was back in a few minutes. I could tell by the look on his face that he hadn't found them.

"They don't seem to be here," Allison said uneasily. "Where else can we look for them?"

I put my head down. I could feel tears welling up in my eyes. I didn't know how we would ever find the calves. They could be wandering anywhere. If they'd broken through a hole in the pen, they could have made the same kind of hole in a fence and be walking right into downtown Acorn Falls by now.

Suddenly I felt strong again. Annabelle was my responsibility. I'd taken on her care, and now she was lost. I had to figure out a plan to find her. So why was I crying? I had to take charge and start thinking!

Quickly I mopped at my face with a tissue I'd found in my jeans pocket. When I looked up, ready to deal with the crisis, Randy was staring at me. Hard.

"What is it, Randy?" I asked. "Something wrong?"

"Uh-uh, Sabs," she said. "Something you did exactly right!"

By now everyone was looking at Randy. "You mind explaining that?" Jason asked.

"It's easy," Randy answered. "We're all wasting our time here. Why should we go out looking for the calves? Why not let the calves find us?"

"Why should they?" Nick asked.

"Because," Randy said with a gleam in her eye, "Sabs taught Annabelle to appreciate good music."

"Randy," Katie said, jumping up, "that's a perfect idea!"

"It really is, Randy," I agreed. I knew exactly what she had in mind.

Ten minutes later everything was ready. "Which song do we try first?" Randy asked me.

I thought about it. Annabelle moved fastest at a trot, and she trotted when she heard the Beatles.

"Play 'I Want to Hold Your Hand,'" I told her.

Randy rummaged through her tapes, which she carried in her backpack, for a Beatles tape and handed it to Jason.

"Here we go," Jason said. He and Nick had rigged up Jason's stereo speakers to connect with his tape deck. They'd brought the whole thing outside and plugged it into an electrical outlet in the barn.

"I sure hope this works," I murmured to Randy as the song started blasting out of the speakers.

"I hope so, too," Randy answered. "I don't have any Petula Clark."

We both started to giggle. It was a big relief to laugh, even though I was so worried. Somehow Randy's idea made me feel hopeful. If anything would bring Annabelle back, this would do it.

The Beatles began to seriously rock. Jason turned the volume up to a roar. I had a feeling everyone in the state could hear it!

Nick had a pair of binoculars in his hand. While the song played, he scanned the area, looking for signs. I was so nervous, I was pacing back and forth in front of the barn. This just had to work!

By the time the song got to the second chorus, though, I was beginning to wonder. Then, all of a sudden, I heard Nick shout, "There they are!"

I ran over to him. He was waving at two tiny figures moving through the shadows. I grabbed the binoculars and focused on them. It was Army and Annabelle!

I was so happy to see Annabelle, I ran all the way down the hill to hug her. She looked up at me lazily, as though she couldn't imagine what all the fuss was about. She nuzzled against me as I stroked her ears. "Oh, Annabelle, where were you?" I asked.

She nuzzled closer. I realized then that it didn't matter. All that really mattered was that Annabelle was finally home.

Chapter Eight

It wasn't until we took the calves into the barn that I realized Annabelle must have had a terrific time on her morning out. She had yellow and green stains all over her body. It looked like she'd been rolling around in the grass for hours.

"Oh, no!" I said in despair. "How will I ever get her clean?"

Jason looked as relieved over Army as I was over Annabelle. Now he came over to inspect Annabelle. "She does look pretty grungy," he agreed. He looked at Nick, then at Randy, Katie, and Al. "I guess we'll have to make a party of it!" he went on.

"Or a contest." Nick grinned.

I looked at him. He'd been so great while we were worried about the calves. Was he going to make fun of me now? "What kind of contest?" I asked. "Boys against girls?"

Nick pretended to consider it. Then he shook his head. "No way," he said finally. "I have a feeling Jason and I would lose to you girls big-time."

I couldn't believe it! He was smiling at me. Somehow, I knew that the teasing was over for good. I'd obviously proven myself to him, and he wasn't going to make fun of me for not being as good as a boy. Now I could get Annabelle ready for the fair without wondering if Nick really hated me or would ever talk to me again.

We decided to have our picnic first and then get down to cleaning the cows. Jason's eyes sparkled when Allison lifted out her cherry pie. "I can't wait for dessert!" he announced. We all burst out laughing.

"So, what are you all going to do at the fair?" Nick asked as we set up a tablecloth under a big tree.

"Everybody's getting involved," I said proudly. "Katie's entering her quilting block for the big 4-H quilt, and Allison's entering the pie contest."

"What about Randy?" Nick asked as he reached for a piece of cold fried chicken that Jason's mom had supplied.

I glanced at Randy, but she shook her head. "Oh, that's a secret," I said mysteriously.

"A secret?" Nick asked. "Why? Can't I even have a hint?"

Randy's eyes were sparkling. "Well, okay, a little hint," I said. I looked at the others. They all looked like they were ready to explode with laughter. "Let's say . . . it has something to do with rap music."

"Rap music?" Nick repeated. He looked completely bewildered.

"What does rap music have to do with a country fair?" Jason asked, helping himself to some potato chips.

"You'll see tomorrow!" Randy promised.

"This should be good," Nick said to Jason.

"Definitely worth seeing," Jason agreed. "Right now, though, I want to check out Allison's pie."

"First slice goes to Jason," Allison announced as she cut her latest pie with a flourish.

"Be careful, Jason," Randy warned him. "Allison's such an expert by now that she's adding all kinds of nutty ingredients to the recipe. There's no telling what's in this one!"

"I'll take my chances," Jason answered, looking at the pie hungrily. It really did look terrific: Allison had all kinds of little cuts and fork pricks in it, just like all the good pies I'd ever seen.

Jason took a heaping forkful and stuffed it into his mouth. The happiest expression came over his face. He chewed very, very slowly and swallowed. Then he just sat there grinning, not saying a word.

"Well, what do you think?" Katie asked him. "You think it's worth a ribbon?"

Jason looked over at Allison, who was busy cutting slices for everyone else. "Allison?" he asked. "This is awesome! I could swear there's chocolate in this pie."

"There is," Allison admitted.

We all stopped eating our chicken and cut into the pie. Allison watched as we ate.

When I'd swallowed my first bite, I couldn't believe it! This was the best cherry pie I'd ever tasted in my life! There was this great milk chocolate taste under the cherries, which gave the whole pie a flavor that was out of this world!

"It's a winner, Al!" I said excitedly. "Don't

change a thing about this recipe! They're going to go out of their minds at the fair tomorrow!"

"It's the best one yet," Katie agreed, finishing off her slice.

"Definitely hot," Randy added. "Nobody would ever believe you couldn't bake a pie a week ago!"

Allison smiled. "Let's hope I can do exactly the same thing tomorrow," she said.

"Speaking of tomorrow . . ." Jason finished his pie and got up. "We'd better get going if we want the calves to be ready for the fair." He nodded at my friends. "Just wait right here," he told them. "Sabrina will tell you what to do."

I felt really good hearing that from Jason. It sounded like I was totally in control of things, like he had confidence in me. I tried to act casual but confident. "I'll get her into the washrack," I told them. "Then we can give her a good scrubbing and clip her."

It took hours to wash and groom Annabelle. Even though I had three helpers, and Jason and Nick worked together on Army, it seemed to take forever.

Finally I stood back and looked at Annabelle from all sides. "What's wrong, Sabs?" Katie asked. "We clipped her just like you told us to."

"And my hands are sore from washing her," Randy added. "What else do we have to do?"

I looked at Annabelle's sides. There was no way around it. I could still see those awful stains. No judge was going to give a ribbon to a calf that looked black and white and *yellow*!

I looked at the soap in the washrack. There was only a sliver left. We'd used almost a whole cake, and Annabelle was still yellow. The soap just wasn't going to be enough. I had to find something else to get rid of those stains.

Nick came over to inspect Annabelle. "You did a great job!" he said.

I still couldn't believe how much his attitude toward me had changed. When he smiled at me like that, something inside me melted.

"Thanks," I replied. "We've all been working really hard. But I still have to get those stains off of her sides."

"What if we can't get the stains out?" Randy asked. "Are you going to show her like this?"

Jason came over. I showed him the stains on Annabelle. "What do I do about these?" I wanted to know.

He grinned at me. "I shouldn't help you at

all," he warned me. "After all, we are competing against each other."

"Jason!" I wailed. "What am I going to do if you don't give me some ideas? Annabelle will never get clean enough to win!"

"Well, all right," he said. He looked at her body, then at the tiny piece of soap we had left. "You can't wash those stains out tonight, that's for sure," he said thoughtfully.

"Then what should I do?" I asked him. "It'll be bright and sunny tomorrow. The judges will see everything."

"I know," he answered. "But just because you can't get her clean doesn't mean you can't cover up the stains."

"Cover them up?" I asked. This sounded kind of interesting. "Cover them up how?"

Jason grinned at me. "Some people use white paint," he said.

"Paint?" Katie squeaked. "On an animal?"

Jason nodded. "It won't hurt her," he told me. "Honest. And you can use white paint on her body as long as you don't try to cover up a black spot with white. That's illegal at 4-H. We've got some paint behind the barn, if you want it," he offered.

91

I thought about that. I hated the idea of putting paint on Annabelle, contest or no contest. It just didn't seem right to paint an animal.

Katie saw me looking at the calf. "You don't want to do it, do you?" she asked quietly. Sometimes Katie knows just what I'm feeling. It's a big comfort.

I shook my head. "It seems cruel. I wouldn't want someone painting me," I answered.

"How about using something you might use on yourself?" Randy suggested.

"Like what?" I asked.

"Well . . . milk, maybe. Or some kind of hair bleach," Randy offered. "You wouldn't think twice about using that on yourself."

She was right. I actually had used a sort of bleach once, to try and win the lead in the Bradley production of *Grease*. Randy had come to the rescue when my hair turned orange. Bleach would lighten the stains until they hardly showed at all, and I wouldn't mind using it on Annabelle.

"Okay," I agreed, "let's bleach them out."

Randy went to the McKees' house for some household bleach. Meanwhile, Katie and Allison helped me put away the clippers and washcloths we'd used on Annabelle. It was getting late, and I was so tired, I was ready to topple over. But it would be worth it, if we could bleach out those stains. Then we could all go home and rest up for the fair the next day.

Randy came back with a big bottle of bleach, and I knelt next to Annabelle, singing softly to her as I poured some on a fresh washcloth. "Let's hope this works," I said as I started to scrub at the stains.

As soon as I rubbed the bleach on, the stains started to fade. I kept rubbing and rubbing, and soon Annabelle looked like she'd spent the whole day in the pen. I washed the bleach off thoroughly so she wouldn't lick any of it.

"Great job, Sabs!" Allison said, walking around the washrack. "You can't see a thing."

"Better keep a bottle of that handy tomorrow," Katie warned me. "Just in case Annabelle decides to roll around her pen tonight."

"Great idea, Katie," I agreed. "I'm not going anywhere without my secret weapon!"

I looked proudly at Annabelle. She was all ready for the fair. By tomorrow night, we'd know whether she really was a champion!

Chapter Nine

My friends stayed over at my house on Saturday night, and on Sunday we all headed over to the fair together. Once we got there, Allison had to hurry off to set up for the baking contest. Randy went with her to give her some last-minute advice. Katie and I walked around trying to see everything at once. Luckily, Jason and his parents were bringing Annabelle and Army from the farm, so I could spend some time just enjoying the fair. The cow judging wasn't until later in the afternoon.

There was so much to do and see at the fair! There was an entire section of nothing but farm animals — horses, pigs, goats, cows — in their own barns near the back of the fairgrounds. There were judges for each separate category, and you could see them walking through the exhibits, marking clipboards, and talking to each other in low voices.

There was also a big crafts section. That's where a lot of people were gathering now. They had old-fashioned crafts, like spinning thread at a spinning wheel and painting china, and all kinds of modern crafts. It was almost time for the quilting exhibit, so we stopped at the crafts booth. About thirty contestants were already there.

"Good luck, Katie!" I called to her as she headed off to the platform. I could tell she was nervous. She was clutching her quilt block tightly in both hands. Because quilting took so much time, the contestants had done their blocks at home and brought them in for judging.

The judging was about to begin. Six women were sitting at a table on a raised platform, with pads and pencils in front of them. Each contestant had to take out her quilt block and show it to each of the judges. Then the contestant put the quilt block in a pile with the others and walked off.

Even I was getting nervous as I watched each contestant walk through the line of judges. Katie must have been really scared. She was almost at the end of the line, and I could see her legs trembling a little when she finally walked across the platform with her block. She laid it carefully in front of each judge, who nodded and marked her pad. When she finally reached the end of the line, she told the head judge her name and left her quilt block on the pile.

I gave Katie a hug when she came down off the platform. "That looked really awful, Katie!" I said.

"It was pretty intense," Katie agreed. "I can't believe how scared I was just walking past a table!"

"When do they announce the winners?" I asked.

Katie looked at her watch. "They told us to come back in an hour," she told me. "We have time to go watch Allison in the pie-baking contest, if we hurry."

We circled around the crafts section, sniffing the air. When we finally started smelling cherries, I knew we were really close.

"There it is!" Katie pointed. "And there's Randy, right in front!"

We hurried over to join Randy, who was watching Allison, standing at a long table with a number of other contestants. "Take it easy,

Al," Randy was telling her in a loud voice. She wanted to make sure Stacy the Great, standing a few feet away, heard everything. "You've got this contest sewn up. Nobody else stands a chance."

"Is that so?" Stacy sneered. "Why don't you forfeit right now, Allison? That way, you'll spare yourself unnecessary embarrassment. My parents think my cherry pie should be world-famous!"

"That's why they're your parents," Randy shot back. "You know what they say — 'A pie only a mother could love'!"

Stacy was so mad, she had to bite her lip to keep from saying anything else. I think Randy definitely won that round. "Nice going, Ran," I told her when I reached her. "You sure left her speechless."

"And Al's job is to leave her ribbonless!" Randy said with a grin. "How about it, Al? Are you all set?"

"I'm a little nervous," Allison admitted. "I just hope it comes out the way it did yesterday."

"If it does, you'll win by a mile," Katie assured her. "Just hang in there and relax. You'll be fine."

"All right, contestants," came a woman's voice. "We're ready to start now. Each of you will use your own recipe. We provide the ingredients. Please stand at your stations, and remember not to take anything from any other contestant. On your mark — get set — go!"

Allison and the others went right to work, picking out fresh cherries and stirring up other ingredients in big bowls. I could see Al was working a little more slowly than the others, trying to remember everything in her recipe and not make any mistakes. The contestants only had a few minutes to get their ingredients ready for the oven, and Al was being so careful, I began to wonder whether she'd get everything finished in time to put it in the oven. If she didn't, the pie wouldn't have as long to bake as the others.

"Come on, Al!" I urged her. "You can do it!" We weren't allowed to yell out anything about her recipe, or she would be disqualified, but I kept hoping she'd remember to add as much chocolate as she had for the pie we ate at the picnic. It surprised me to realize that I was actually hoping to taste this pie when it came out of the oven!

I could see the clock behind them ticking away. There were only five minutes left to prepare the entire crust, fill it with the cherries, and pinch it together. Stacy was working really fast. She had the top crust almost in place on her pie. Allison hadn't even finished spooning in her filling yet!

"Hurry, Al!" I called to her.

But Allison just couldn't speed up. She was more concerned with getting it right than beating everyone else on the oven time. Her pie was the last one into the oven. She was at least ten minutes behind everyone else.

"The pies will now bake for fifty minutes," announced the woman judge. "Then we'll take them out and taste them. Contestants, you may be excused. Come back in an hour and a half for the judging."

Allison came down to meet us on the grass. She wore a huge apron, which was covered with cherry stains. She looked exhausted. "I think I remembered it right," she told us. "But it won't bake as long as the others."

"Hey, don't worry about it," Randy said to comfort her. "If you got it right, that's all that counts. We all know it's a winner, don't we?"

"Absolutely!" I said. "Al, I didn't think I could look at another cherry pie until I tried the one you made yesterday. Now I'm dying for another piece!"

Allison smiled at me. "Sabs, you're the greatest," she said.

Katie glanced at her watch. "Hey, I've got to get back to the quilting exhibit! It's time for the judges' announcement!"

We all ran through the crowd to get back to the quilting exhibit. The head judge had a list in her hand, and she was already standing at the microphone when we finally got there. "We've got some beautiful quilt blocks from this year's contestants," she said. "It was really tough for the judges to single out the twelve whose blocks will be sewn into the Bradley quilt. However, we do have the names of our winners. Will each of you please step forward as I call your name."

The judge read off one name after another. One by one, the contestants stepped forward and smiled at the applause. I could hardly stand the suspense as eight, nine, ten names were called. Finally there were only two more places on the quilt block.

The judge looked down at her list. "And the eleventh winner is . . . Jamie Howell! Congratulations, Jamie!"

Katie bit her lip. "Hey, it's okay, Katie," I said, hoping to cheer her up. "There's still one more place."

Katie nodded, but she still didn't look very happy.

The judge adjusted the microphone. "And for our twelfth and last winner, the last block in our Bradley quilt comes from —" I held my breath — "Miss Katherine Campbell! Congratulations, Katherine!"

That was Katie! I screamed and jumped up and down. Katie had tears in her eyes, she was so happy. She stepped forward, nodded at the applause, and stood back. Randy and Allison were clapping so hard, it sounded like thunder in my ears.

"You're a winner, Katie!" I cried. "I'm so proud of you!"

"That's our first prize at the fair," said Allison.

"Which leaves three to go," added Randy.

We giggled at her for being so sure we'd all win prizes. We walked around the crafts section for a little while, staying close to the baking booth so we could be there in time for the judging.

Finally it was time. We went to the booth and found that all the pies had been taken out of the oven and lined up on long tables, with the bakers' names in front. It smelled absolutely incredible in that tent. My mouth was watering! We found Allison's pie and stood as close to it as we could. Allison went to stand behind the table.

I looked at Allison's pie and then at the other pies next to it. It seemed, somehow, like Allison's pie was a little lighter in color than the others.

"She needed more baking time," Katie said to me quietly. So that was it. Her pie crust hadn't had enough time to get really golden, the way it was the day before.

"That's okay," I said, trying to sound confident. "Her recipe's so great, it'll still beat everything else there."

The contestants stood quietly next to their pies as the judges came down the row, sniffing and tasting each one. Allison smiled bravely at us, but I could tell she wasn't happy about the way hers had turned out.

When they'd tasted all the pies, the judges went into a huddle at the back of the exhibit. The contestants came down from the platform to stand with their friends and family.

"It was perfect," I heard Stacy say to Eva and B.Z. "The best pie I ever made." She turned around and spotted Allison. "Oh, Allison," she said sweetly, "sorry about your little problem. You needed more oven time, didn't you? That can really ruin a pie."

Allison looked crushed, but she didn't say a word. I got mad that Stacy was making fun of her. But there was nothing I could do except give Allison a hug.

"Thanks, Sabs," she said. "It really helps to have somebody on your side, especially when Stacy the Great is around!"

The head judge stepped to the edge of the platform. "We're ready with our decisions," she announced. "We'll be giving a third-, second-, and first-place ribbon, and then a special mention."

We were so nervous, we couldn't say anything. The judge continued, "The third place ribbon goes to . . . Dick Sommers!"

A tall, thin boy I didn't know stepped forward and grinned. He was the only boy in the competition, and I thought it was great that he'd won a place. The judge handed him a yellow ribbon, and he waved at the crowd.

"Second place," the judge announced. I could feel my throat getting tighter and tighter. "The second-place ribbon goes to . . . Leslie Morton! Congratulations, Leslie!" Leslie stepped forward, waved to the crowd, and climbed up on the platform to accept her pink ribbon.

"First place," came the judge's voice. I couldn't look at Allison. "We have a two-way tie for first place!"

Oh, no, I thought. Allison and Stacy won the blue ribbon together! I couldn't stand it, especially after Randy had bragged about Allison's great baking!

Allison was clenching her hands together. "The blue ribbons go to . . . Wendy Leiter and Stacy Hansen!"

A big cheer went up. I felt sick. Oh, no! Allison didn't win a place at all! Stacy was already bowing to the crowd, and then she ran up on the platform and took the blue ribbon from the judges. I tried not to look. As Stacy came down, she gave Allison this sickening smile. I was furious.

The judge was back at the microphone. "Now for our special mention," she continued. "We don't do it every year, but this year we're going to award a ribbon for best original recipe. There were a lot of great pies this year, but one was truly outstanding. It was a creative and exciting new way to bake a cherry pie. So this year's best original recipe award goes to . . . Allison Cloud!"

We screamed like crazy! I was so happy, I was actually crying. Katie had tears in her eyes, too. Allison looked dazed. In fact, she couldn't move at all until I pushed her toward the platform. Finally she stumbled up the steps and took the blue ribbon from the judges.

We were all admiring the ribbon when Katie glanced at her watch. "Hey, we can't forget about Annabelle," she reminded me. "Your event's starting any minute."

She was right! We had to rush to get to the barn on time.

Chapter Ten

When we got to the dairy barn, Jason and his family had already unloaded Annabelle. I just had to get her cleaned up, touch up her grooming, and have her ready to show. I had about half an hour before the competition started. An entire flock of butterflies was flittering around in my stomach. I was so nervous!

Annabelle was quiet, and I could tell she was happy. When I stroked her ears, she nuzzled right next to me, just like she always did, and when I sang her a chorus of "Downtown," her ears perked right up. She was listening to me and ready to do whatever I wanted.

I'd kept the bottle of bleach with me, and I used it quickly to rub off a few new stains she'd gotten on her coat. Then I gave her a long, thorough brushing with a curry brush and checked her from head to toe. I checked Annabelle for extra hairs to clip and kept finding a few more.

Jason, who was working next to me with Army, knew just how I felt. "Take it easy, Sabrina," he said. "The way you keep clipping, there won't be any Annabelle left for the show!"

I was really surprised when I saw Nick walk up to the stall we'd been assigned. "Just wanted to say good luck," he told me, blushing a little. "I think you've done a great job with Annabelle."

"Thanks, Nick," I said, feeling really good inside. I almost didn't care now if I won a place or not. Nick thought I had done a great job. I had convinced him that I knew what I was doing. To me, that meant more than a blue ribbon!

A loud voice came over the P.A. and told us to take our calves out to the pen for the judging. This was the big moment. "Good luck," I said to Jason as we snapped halters on our calves.

"Good luck to you, too, Sabs," he replied. "You're a good sport."

Wow! I was getting compliments left and right today! I tried to remember them all as Annabelle and I walked slowly toward the judging pen. One by one, we were told to take our calves into the pen and lead for the judges.

"Sabrina Wells and Annabelle!" came a voice above me.

Okay, Sabs, this is it, I told myself. You can do it. "Come on, Annabelle," I whispered to my calf. "Let's show 'em how it's done."

I stepped into the ring. "Stand, please," called the judge. Right away, I started to sing "Summer Nights" very softly. Annabelle stood still.

"Thank you. Now walk, please," said the judge.

I turned to Annabelle and started to sing the words to "Downtown." She immediately stepped out into a nice walk. She moved like a dancer. Well, like a dancer with four legs who eats grain and hay.

I could tell the judges were a little surprised by my instructions. But it was working perfectly, and I knew Annabelle felt comfortable and happy.

"Will you have her trot, please?" asked the judge.

Now I turned to Annabelle and sang a Beatles tune. Annabelle broke into the best trot she'd ever done. I was so proud of her! How could the judges not think she was the best calf at the fair?

Finally it was over. It seemed to take forever before the judge stepped forward with a paper in his hand. Third place went to some guy I'd never met. He beamed as he accepted the ribbon from the judge.

"Second place," called the judge, "goes to . . . Jason McKee and Army!"

We all yelled for Jason. He was so excited, he could hardly walk through the crowd to accept his ribbon. He gave Army a huge hug when he came back.

"And now, first place — and incidentally, not only a blue ribbon, but also this year's Dairy Princess," the judge said solemnly. We all looked at each other. I clenched my hands so tight, I was afraid I might break a bone. "The girl chosen to represent the dairy industry at local PTAs and student groups — a very high honor indeed to a brand-new calf-raiser — the blue ribbon goes to . . . Miss Sabrina Wells and Annabelle!"

Ohmygosh! I was so excited, I started to cry. In fact, I couldn't seem to stop. I really wanted to smile and wave to everyone, but I was so full of emotion that it was just pouring out of me.

I could see Nick right behind me as I turned to pick up the ribbon. He was smiling and cheering with everyone else. I stumbled through the crowd to pick up the blue ribbon and thank the judges. But the truth is, I would have been happy even without the blue ribbon. It was just so great to know that I had done what I had set out to do. And now everyone knew it!

I gave Annabelle a big hug. Without her it would have been impossible. She's the best calf in the world!

Once I had put Annabelle back into her pen with Army, my friends and I headed over to the big barn. It was time for Randy's event.

The big sign outside the barn read SQUARE DANCE. There were already lots of people there. They were all dressed up in country-style clothes, waiting for the music to start so they could dance. I looked around but couldn't find Randy.

"There she is!" Katie said, pointing to a group of people sitting next to the bandstand. "I guess those are the other contestants, too."

We all burst out laughing. The other contestants were wearing scarves around their necks, cowboy hats, silver belt buckles, and Western boots. Randy was sitting calmly in her black lace-up granny boots, tight black biker shorts, a tie-dyed tank top, and a baggy, multicolored, sequined shirt tied loosely over it. She had plastic black bracelets from her wrists to her elbows. There was nothing at all "country" about Randy Zak!

"Get into your squares, dancers," announced a jolly voice. It came from a large man up on the stage. He looked like a cowboy — from his ten-gallon hat right down to the spurs on his boots. "We'll be starting our contest in just a moment."

Randy and the other contestants stood up and stretched. The others looked a little nervous. Randy looked as calm as if she was watching the contest, not competing in it.

"All right, dancers," came the judge's voice again. "Just follow the instructions of the caller. Remember, we're judging our square-dance callers on style, knowledge, and ability to keep the dance moving. So do what they tell you, and have a great time! Can we have our first caller, please?" he asked, turning to the contestants.

111

Nick and Jason turned to me with their mouths open.

"Randy's calling a square dance?" Nick asked.

"Yup," I said. "Wait until you hear her. She's really awesome."

"But you said it had something to do with rap," said Jason. "What does square dancing have to do with rap?"

"Just wait and see," Katie said with a giggle as the musicians started tuning up.

The first boy in line stepped forward. He took several deep breaths and nodded to the band behind him. The musicians started to play, and the boy stepped to the microphone. "Okay, let's allemande left and do-si-do," he called. He tapped his foot to the rhythm of the music and moved his hands, too.

The judge gave him two minutes of calling, then asked for the next contestant. This time it was a girl, and she did a lot of the same things the boy did.

"Boy, Randy's going to be a real surprise to all these people," I whispered to Allison.

Allison nodded. "I sure hope they're ready for her," she whispered back.

Finally the contestant before Randy ended his turn. Randy was next. There was a murmur when she stepped to the microphone. "We're going to take this next dance real fast!" she called to the dancers. "Stay with me, okay?"

She nodded to the band, and they started their next song. Randy leaned into the microphone and started to rap, swaying to the music and tapping her foot:

"I'm the coolest caller you've all ever seen —

"You might think I was really just a part of a dream —

"But I'm here to guide you left and right —

"Turn 'round real quick and step real light —

"Swing your partners once 'round and back —

"And now turn away for the grand right-and-left.

"Remember to bow at each guy in the line —

"Then back to your place and time for you to shine."

I looked around at the barn, which was packed with people watching the contest. Nobody could believe Randy! Not only was she giving all the dance instructions in rap, but she was also talking faster than anyone thought was possible! And still she was so clear that the dancers followed right along. They were all nodding and laughing as they danced. It was clear everybody was having a great time with Randy's calling! They all stopped and applauded like crazy when she was done. Randy gave a quick nod and sat down again.

I felt sorry for the last caller. He was so nervous after hearing Randy that he could hardly remember the dance instructions, and he got out of rhythm with the band halfway through. He was really sweating when he finally finished.

The judge stepped to the microphone. "Well, ladies and gentlemen, we have some fine callers from Bradley. But we've got only one ribbon to give out, and clearly that ribbon goes to the most original, most unusual caller I've ever heard. The blue ribbon for the square-dance calling goes to . . . Randy Zak!"

We all cheered and yelled as loud as we could. I couldn't believe it! All three of my friends had taken prizes at the Bradley fair! I was so happy, I could hardly stand it. Randy came back, grinning, with her blue ribbon. "This was all your idea, Al," she said. "If you hadn't come up with the idea, I never would have thought to try it."

"You looked great up there," I told her. "Was it fun?"

"Yeah, it was," Randy answered, sounding a little surprised. "I had no idea country could be so hip!"

Just then the man who had given out the prize came up to us.

"Miss Zak?" he asked. "How would you like to call the first dance tonight?"

"Are you kidding? I'd love to!" Randy exclaimed. She clipped the ribbon to her belt, ran up to the platform, and started talking to the band.

Nick turned to me. He had a really odd expression on his face. "Sabrina, I just wanted to apologize for acting like a jerk lately. You've done amazing things with Annabelle, and I think that you're the best Dairy Princess Bradley's ever had."

I couldn't believe it. He was being so sweet! "Thanks, Nick," I said. "I did feel a little silly with Annabelle at first, but now we're great friends."

"Like us?" he asked.

"Yeah, like us," I said with a smile. My stomach was turning somersaults.

"So, do you want to be my square-dance partner, partner?" Nick asked.

"Yee-ha, partner," I answered. "Let's go!"

We grabbed hands and rushed out onto the dance floor. Allison and her partner, Billy, along with Katie, who was dancing with my brother Sam, had already started to make a square, so we joined them.

The music started, and Randy's voice came out loud and clear over the P.A. "Okay, everybody, grab your partners, and get ready for the rappin'est square dance you've ever heard."

Nick gave me a big grin. I smiled back, and we started to swing our way around the square. This had to be the best 4-H Fair ever!

Don't Miss
Girl Talk # 37
RANDY'S BIG DREAM

"Oh, no, not that song *again*!" I groaned and fell backward onto my bed. "I think this D.J. is trying to brainwash us!"

"Either that, or he's lost some of his CDs," said one of my best friends, Sabrina Wells. "It's the third time he's played that one in less than an hour."

Sabrina was sitting on the floor with my other two best friends, Allison Cloud and Katie Campbell. It was Saturday night, and we were hanging out at my house for a sleepover.

Sabs was twisting Allison's long black hair into a perfect french braid, while Katie lay on her sleeping bag, bouncing a beach ball against my bedroom wall.

"These radio stations are really dumb," Katie said as she tried to spin the ball on her index finger. "Just because a song is popular doesn't mean kids want to hear it a million times in one day."

"And I can't believe there's only one real radio station in Acorn Falls," I moaned. "In New

York —"

"Uh, oh —" Katie warned the others with a teasing grin. "Randy's going to tell us about New York again!"

Katie was right. It was one of those times when I couldn't help comparing life in Acorn Falls to what I had been used to when I lived in New York City — especially when it came to radio stations.

TALK BACK!
TELL US WHAT YOU THINK ABOUT
GIRL TALK BOOKS

Name _____

Address _____

City _____ State _____ Zip_____

Birthday _____ Mo._____ Year _____

Telephone Number (____)_____

1) Did you like this GIRL TALK book?

Check one: YES_____ NO_____

2) Would you buy another GIRL TALK book?

Check one: YES_____ NO_____

If you like GIRL TALK books, please answer questions 3-5; otherwise go directly to question 6.

3) What do you like most about GIRL TALK books?

Check one: Characters_____ Situations_____
        Telephone Talk_____Other_____

4) Who is your favorite GIRL TALK character?

Check one: Sabrina_____ Katie_____ Randy_____
Allison_____ Stacy_____ Other (give name) _____

5) Who is your *least* favorite character?

_____

6) Where did you buy this GIRL TALK book?

Check one: Bookstore____Toy store____Discount store____
Grocery store___Supermarket___Other (give name)_____

Please turn over to continue survey.

7) How many GIRL TALK books have you read?
Check one: 0____   1 to 2____   3 to 4 ____   5 or more____

8) In what type of store would you look for GIRL TALK books?
Bookstore_____Toy store_____Discount store_____
Grocery store____Supermarket_____Other (give name)_____

9) Which type of store would you visit most often if you wanted to buy a GIRL TALK book?
Check *only* one: Bookstore_____Toy store_____
Discount store_____Grocery store_____Supermarket_____
Other (give name)_____

10) How many books do you read in a month?
Check one: 0____   1 to 2____   3 to 4 ____   5 or more____

11) Do you read any of these books?
Check those you have read:
The Baby-sitters Club_____   Nancy Drew_____
Pen Pals_____   Sweet Valley High _____
Sweet Valley Twins_____Gymnasts_____

12) Where do you shop most often to buy these books?
Check one: Bookstore_____Toy store_____
Discount store_____Grocery store_____Supermarket_____
Other (give name)_____

13) What other kinds of books do you read most often?
_____

14) What would you like to read more about in GIRL TALK?
_____
_____

Send completed form to :
GIRL TALK Survey, Western Publishing Company, Inc.
1220 Mound Avenue, Mail Station #85
Racine, Wisconsin 53404

**LOOK FOR THE AWESOME GIRL TALK BOOKS IN
A STORE NEAR YOU!**

Fiction
  #1 WELCOME TO JUNIOR HIGH!
  #2 FACE-OFF!
  #3 THE NEW YOU
  #4 REBEL, REBEL
  #5 IT'S ALL IN THE STARS
  #6 THE GHOST OF EAGLE MOUNTAIN
  #7 ODD COUPLE
  #8 STEALING THE SHOW
  #9 PEER PRESSURE
  #10 FALLING IN LIKE
  #11 MIXED FEELINGS
  #12 DRUMMER GIRL
  #13 THE WINNING TEAM
  #14 EARTH ALERT!
  #15 ON THE AIR
  #16 HERE COMES THE BRIDE
  #17 STAR QUALITY
  #18 KEEPING THE BEAT
  #19 FAMILY AFFAIR
  #20 ROCKIN' CLASS TRIP
  #21 BABY TALK
  #22 PROBLEM DAD
  #23 HOUSE PARTY
  #24 COUSINS
  #25 HORSE FEVER
  #26 BEAUTY QUEENS
  #27 PERFECT MATCH
  #28 CENTER STAGE
  #29 FAMILY RULES
  #30 THE BOOKSHOP MYSTERY
  #31 IT'S A SCREAM!
  #32 KATIE'S CLOSE CALL
  #33 RANDY AND THE *PERFECT* BOY

MORE GIRL TALK TITLES TO LOOK FOR

#34 ALLISON, SHAPE UP!
#35 KATIE AND SABRINA'S BIG COMPETITION
#36 SABRINA AND THE CALF-RAISING DISASTER
#37 RANDY'S BIG DREAM
#38 ALLISON TO THE RESCUE!
#39 KATIE AND THE IMPOSSIBLE COUSINS
#40 SABRINA WINS BIG!
#41 RANDY AND THE GREAT CANOE RACE
#42 ALLISON'S BABY-SITTING ADVENTURE
#43 KATIE'S BEVERLY HILLS FRIEND
#44 RANDY'S BIG CHANCE
#45 SABRINA AND TOO MANY BOYS

Nonfiction

ASK ALLIE 101 answers to your questions about boys, friends, family, and school!

YOUR PERSONALITY QUIZ Fun, easy quizzes to help you discover the real you!

BOYTALK: HOW TO TALK TO YOUR FAVORITE GUY